# in the

# MEADOW

## *Pippa Parker Mysteries: 4*

*Liz Hedgecock*

ISBN-13: 978-1790411948

*For Stephen,*
*who always buys me a beer*
*of my very own*

# CHAPTER 1

Pippa Parker turned her Mini into the drive of Laurel Villa and parked neatly. She got out, savouring the crisp September breeze which ruffled her hair just enough to be pleasant and not irritating. But she couldn't get over the feeling that something was missing.

Something was.

Two somethings, to be precise.

Freddie's absence she was used to. He had been going to preschool on a Monday for months now, and Pippa was happy to wave him off at the door and watch him plop down on the rug and become absorbed in a game, or a book. Today, though, was different.

Today, she had dropped Ruby off first.

Today was the beginning of an experiment.

Today had already been quite stressful, and she hadn't even started yet.

The fun had begun at seven o'clock, when Simon's alarm went off. Freddie had appeared in the doorway almost immediately, as if summoned. 'Is it today?' he asked, his teddy dangling from one hand.

'Is what today?' asked Pippa, fighting the urge to burrow deeper under the covers.

'Is it today that Ruby's going to Granma to be minded?'

'Oh. Oh yes. Yes, it is.'

'I'll go and tell her,' said Freddie.

'No!' yelped Pippa, but he had already vanished, his footsteps thudding down the landing.

'Get up Ruby, you're going to Granma's today!' he cried.

Simon propped himself up on one elbow and ran a hand through his hair, which stood on end. 'I'll go and make tea,' he said, resignedly. As his feet hit the floor, a squeaky giggle erupted from Ruby's room. 'There she blows.'

'Mum! Ruby's nappy needs changing!' bellowed Freddie. 'She smells!'

'Thank you so much,' said Pippa. She threw back the covers and padded to Ruby's room, where the cause of the trouble was standing up in her cot and grinning, possibly because Freddie was tickling her under the chin. 'Good morning, Ruby.'

Ruby turned big blue eyes on her and Pippa's heart melted. 'Goo,' she said, solemnly.

Freddie spent a productive fifteen minutes getting in everyone's way until Pippa gave in and made breakfast. That kept him seated for five minutes, but the moment his spoon clattered into the bowl he was off his seat and heading upstairs. 'We need to pack for Ruby,' he flung over his shoulder.

'Freddie,' called Pippa. 'She's going for the morning, not a week.'

'She still NEEDS THINGS,' he yelled.

Ruby bashed her spoon on the tray of her highchair in agreement. Unfortunately the spoon was fully loaded with banana porridge. Pippa gritted her teeth as yellowish gluey blobs flew around the vicinity, prised the spoon from Ruby's sticky grasp, and reloaded it. 'Your mouth's that way, Rubes.'

Ruby stared at the spoon as if she had never seen anything like it in her life. 'Come on, you know what to do,' said Pippa, taking Ruby's hand and guiding the spoon towards her mouth. Ruby opened wide, and the spoon went in. 'Clamp down,' said Pippa, barely daring to breathe. She did, and Pippa drew the spoon out as if defusing a bomb.

'I've got all your favourite toys, Ruby!' shouted Freddie, running into the room. Ruby grinned in utter adoration, and the porridge dribbled down her babygro.

*Three more hours*, thought Pippa. *Three more hours until peace and quiet.*

And now she had peace and quiet, and the prospect of two hours alone at home, working undisturbed, it felt wrong.

Pippa let herself into Laurel Villa, closed the door, and leaned against it. In the middle of the hall floor were the various items which Freddie had 'packed' for Ruby and Pippa had rejected. Most of these were toys which made a loud noise, since Pippa didn't want the first occasion of Sheila looking after Ruby in a work context to also be the last. Pippa sidestepped them, went to the kitchen and switched on the kettle. She would begin with tea. Tea would help.

The house seemed unnaturally quiet; even the clack of the mug on the worktop practically echoed. The fridge door clunked menacingly. The clock ticked, and Pippa tried not to feel guilty at every tock, every grain of sand slipping through the hourglass, every second which ought to be productively spent in freelance event organisation and PR, and which she was currently spending watching a kettle boil.

*A watched kettle never boils*, Pippa told herself. *I should go and do something else.* Yet she was still leaning on the worktop, watching it like a cat watches a mouse hole in a cartoon. Because if she lifted the lid of the laptop waiting for her in the dining room, fully charged, with a notebook and pen by its side, her to-do list would be there, looking at her. And she wasn't sure she was ready for it.

Not without tea.

At last the kettle boiled and Pippa drowned the teabag gratefully. Buffy glared from the mug, presumably about to face down a vampire or two and relishing the opportunity. Pippa squeezed the teabag, flicked it into the bin and added milk. *All you have to face is a set of event bookings. You should be grateful.*

She took her mug into the dining room, placed it on a coaster well away from the laptop, and lifted the lid as if she were ripping off a plaster.

*There. That wasn't so bad.*

***

Following the success of the afternoon teas at

Higginbotham Hall, Lady Higginbotham (who always said 'Call me June', but Pippa could never quite bring herself to do it) had summoned Pippa to the hall to discuss ideas.

'What about a play?' asked Beryl Harbottle, as she sliced the marzipan carrot from her slice of cake with surgical precision. 'We could ask the Gadding Players back. People could bring cushions to sit on and we could do open-air theatre.'

Pippa tried not to shudder. 'After the last time?'

Beryl laid down her fork. 'Now Pippa, that wasn't typical. The swords are all in a glass case now, and if you want I'll lock the drawing room and you can have the key.'

'I'd be happier if they did a drawing-room farce,' said Pippa. 'Although then they might have to eat and drink things…' She saw PC Horsley, grim-faced and stoic, taking a sip or a bite of everything before it was allowed on stage. 'I'm not sure… Anyway,' she added, her face brightening, 'what about the weather? You know how rainy it is in the autumn.'

'True,' said Lady Higginbotham wistfully. 'Perhaps next summer.' She gazed into her teacup as if divining the future from its murky brown depths. 'But what can we do now? I don't want people to forget us, and I would like to get the east wing fully watertight before the rain hits.'

Pippa racked her brains for something which didn't involve swords, violence (pretend or otherwise), eating, drinking, or indeed any risk to anyone at all. Who was the safest, most dependable, least melodramatic person she could think of?

Norm swam into her mind, but somehow she didn't

think moving the library to Higginbotham Hall and making it pay-to-enter would be the money spinner Lady Higginbotham was looking for. *Keep searching, Pippa...*

Someone was in her head, just out of reach, and Pippa snapped her fingers to try and summon them. By a miracle, it worked. Jeff, strutting on stage with Short Back and Sides, snapping his fingers and launching into close harmony so sharp it was almost dangerous.

'A series of concerts,' she said dreamily. 'With local performers. We could call it the Much Gadding Proms.'

'Oh *yes*,' breathed Lady Higginbotham, clasping her hands together like a romantic heroine in a black and white film. 'How *suitable*.'

'I'd want them under cover though,' said Pippa. 'Electricity and rain don't mix.'

'But we could have food and drink?' Lady Higginbotham wheedled.

'From approved suppliers, yes,' Pippa conceded.

'Excellent.' Lady Higginbotham rubbed her hands together in a most businesslike way. 'I assume Saturday evenings would work?'

'They would,' said Pippa, mentally waving goodbye to rubbish TV and a bottle of wine with Simon, or possibly a gossip-fest with Lila

'Splendid. Perhaps a series of six?'

'I'll contact a few people first and see what the interest is. Plus I'll need costs for the marquee or stage.'

Beryl sliced her remaining cake neatly in half. 'Oh Pippa, always so cautious.' Her voice held a trace of exasperation.

‘Caution is a good thing,’ said Pippa. ‘I’ll come back to you with more information soon.’

‘A series of proms…’ said June Higginbotham, with a faraway look, and Pippa knew she was hooked.

And now she had to organise it all.

Her first action was a text to Lila. *Would Jeff and SB&S be interested in doing a concert at Higginbotham Hall? P x*

The reply came by return. *Course he would, when? I’ll have to check his calendar. L x*

One act booked. Pippa smiled. Lila wasn’t Jeff’s manager exactly, but since she had discovered Jeff’s secret hobby Short Back and Sides had acquired a website, an email address, a Facebook, Twitter and Instagram presence, and a YouTube channel. Oh, and a regular Thursday evening slot at the posh country pub where Pippa had first met Jeff, The Rambler’s Rest. Would it be tactless to ask if they knew of any other good acts she could book? There were a few contenders from SingFest… She browsed the internet and found three of them, whom she emailed with a tentative enquiry.

Next, marquee or stage. Pippa checked the website of the marquee company she had used for the summer fete. No stages there . . . but would it be safer to have everyone in a big tent? Although that wasn’t exactly a prom. Anyway, she should look at event insurance…

***

Pippa started as her phone alarm shrilled, then felt a pang of guilt that she had gone so far down her research rabbit hole. She saved her spreadsheet, bookmarked every open tab, closed the laptop down properly, and put it away in its shockproof case. Perhaps there would be more time later. Though she doubted it.

Dawn answered the door. 'Ooh hello, Mrs Parker. Freddie's been telling us that his little sister's having an adventure.' She looked puzzled, although for Dawn this was not unusual.

Pippa smiled. 'Oh yes, my mother-in-law has been minding her this morning. Has Freddie been good?'

Dawn's face cleared. 'Oh yes.' She grinned. 'He said he'd packed all her things and said goodbye.'

'Don't worry, I'm fetching her next.'

'Muuuuuummmm!' Freddie barrelled over and winded Pippa with an extravagant hug. 'We had chicken dinosaurs!'

'I always wondered what dinosaurs tasted like, and now I know.' Pippa kissed the top of Freddie's head and ruffled his hair. The doorbell pinged behind her and she turned to answer it. 'Oh, hi Imogen.'

'Hi Pippa.' Imogen's fluffy blonde hair was a little windswept. 'Am I late?'

Pippa shook her head and pointed to the big clock on the wall. 'A whole minute to go.'

'Oh good.' Imogen exhaled. 'I was reading that . . . darn booklet and forgot the time.'

'What darn booklet?'

'You know, the schools admission one.' Imogen tapped the door, which had a poster stuck on the inside of the glass.

'Oh, um, yes,' said Pippa. 'How was it?'

Imogen's eyes widened. 'You haven't read it yet? That makes me feel better. I thought I was the only person in the world who hadn't sent my form in.'

'Henry!' called Dawn. 'Time to go!'

'Ooh yes, I suppose we better had,' said Imogen. 'See you tomorrow, Pippa.'

'Tomorrow?' said Pippa, her mind in a whirl.

'Yes, at playgroup.' Imogen bent to hug Henry.

'Of course,' said Pippa. 'At playgroup. Come along, Freddie, let's go and get your sister.'

'Is she *still* at Granma's?' Freddie said loudly as they stepped outside.

'Um, yes. Wait a minute.' Pippa pretended to rummage in her bag as a cover for peering at the poster on the door.

*ADMISSION TO PRIMARY SCHOOL*

*Was your child born between 1 September 2013 and 31 August 2014?*

Pippa nodded, guiltily.

*If so, he or she is eligible to start primary school in September 2018. Download your Gadcestershire primary schools information booklet from...*

Pippa pulled out her phone and took a picture of the poster, then sighed heavily, took Freddie's hand, and trudged down the path towards the Mini. A new item had barged its way to the front of her to-do list, and she suspected it wouldn't leave her alone until it was done.

# CHAPTER 2

'Oh no, she's been as good as gold,' said Sheila, again. 'Haven't you, Ruby?'

'Ya!' Ruby grinned and crowed from the travel cot in the corner. She looked full of beans, while Sheila looked as if she had been fighting a dragon for the last few hours. Not dishevelled, exactly, but distinctly haggard.

'Ruby can be, um, tiring —'

'We had lots of fun, didn't we Ruby?' Sheila was displaying the slightly manic brightness of someone who really needed a lie down. 'We had a play and then Ruby had her mid-morning drink and snack and I thought she might want a nap but she was too excited to sleep, so we went for a nice long walk round the village in the pram, didn't we? A nice looooong walk.'

'Shall I make you a cup of tea, Sheila?' asked Pippa. 'I bet you haven't had one all morning.'

Sheila's expression wavered between *yes please* and *I can show no weakness*. 'That would be nice,' she said, settling herself a little more firmly on the sofa. 'Freddie can chat to Ruby, can't you dear?'

Freddie was leaning over the side of the travel cot trying to get Ruby's attention, which was currently fixed on a small brass dog on Sheila's mantelpiece.

'They'll be fine,' said Pippa, and went to the kitchen.

When she returned with the tray Sheila's eyes were closed and her mouth open. 'Sheila,' Pippa said, putting the tray down. '*Tea.*'

Sheila's eyes snapped open. 'Did you remember I always have it in a china cup? Oh yes, good.' She leaned forward for her cup. 'Do you know where I keep the biscuits, dear?'

'I'll go and get them,' said Pippa, rising. She had hoped not to tempt the children with biscuits, but it seemed a small price to pay for a morning of comparative freedom.

*Well, being stuck to a laptop.*

'I meant to say,' said Sheila, taking a ginger nut from the plate, 'we went past the meadow.'

'Oh yes?' said Pippa, without interest. The meadow, which stretched from behind the shops on the village green to the river bank, was pretty with wildflowers in the summer, but boggy and overgrown at this point in the year. Plus a big noticeboard by the footpath, courtesy of the Gadding Naturalists' Society, warned anyone who cared to venture onto the meadow that it was a site of botanical interest and they had better not step on any plants or insects in case they damaged the fragile ecosystem. It made Pippa feel like a blundering Gulliver, so she tended to stick to the village green, which was regularly mown, nettle-free, and had benches.

'There was a van,' said Sheila, significantly.

'A van?' said Pippa, because she could tell that Sheila intended it as a cue, and it was the least she could do for a morning of Ruby-sitting.

Sheila nodded in an I-told-you-so kind of way. 'It was parked opposite the church, by the listed cottages. Half on the pavement.'

'Oh dear,' said Pippa, as it seemed expected.

'And do you know what was on the side of the van?'

Pippa felt her role as Sheila's straight woman was becoming a little too predictable, and merely raised her eyebrows.

'I'll tell you.' Sheila put her cup and saucer down with a decisive chink. 'Green Construction.'

'Green Construction?'

'*Exactly,*' said Sheila, with an air that there was nothing more to be said.

'I'm not sure I —'

'Don't you see, Pippa?' Sheila's haggard look had vanished. 'The van can't have been visiting any of the listed cottages, because those are Grade 1 and the council wouldn't allow it. It wasn't to do with the church, or they'd have put it in the car park. And if it was visiting one of the houses past the ford, they'd have parked outside. So that leaves…' She looked at Pippa, who shrugged. 'That leaves the meadow!'

'Or the van man could have been on a tea break, or getting a newspaper, or passing through.'

A faint furrow appeared between Sheila's eyebrows. 'I

know what I think. You're not the only person who can work things out, Pippa.' She sipped her tea, regarding her daughter-in-law over the rim of the cup. Pippa noted the set of Sheila's shoulders and reflected that, while Sheila had never mentioned returning from holiday to find that Pippa had solved a case without her, she hadn't seemed particularly pleased at the news.

'Maybe you're right, Sheila,' she said. 'But why would they be interested in the meadow?'

'Housing,' Sheila said, crisply. 'It's affordable housing here, affordable housing there, and developers sniffing round all over the place. They've made a right mess of Greater Gadding. It used to be a lovely little village and now it's full of townhouses. I mean, there's even a *retail park*.' She made it sound like an abattoir, or possibly a house of ill-repute.

'Well, there's no way a retail park would fit on the meadow,' said Pippa, as soothingly as she could. 'And I doubt they'd get many houses on it.'

'Apartments, then.' Sheila sniffed. 'Luxury apartments, or a, what is it, community for the over-55s. I know their game.'

'I didn't know you felt so strongly about the meadow, Sheila,' Pippa remarked, trying to keep the amusement out of her voice.

'Just you wait.'

Ruby chose that moment to whack her rattle against the side of the travel cot, and Sheila brightened immediately. 'Ruby-poos! We were so busy chatting that we nearly forgot you!'

'I'd better take her home for lunch,' said Pippa. 'Thank you for looking after her, Sheila.'

'It was a pleasure,' said Sheila, with a slightly guarded expression. 'Although of course I am quite busy, you know.'

'Could you manage once a week?' asked Pippa. 'I got lots done today, and it was a big help.'

Relief washed over Sheila's face. 'Oh yes, once a week is fine.'

'I wouldn't want to wear you out —'

'Wear me out? I'm a spring chicken!' said Sheila, with somewhat forced gaiety. 'Same time next week!'

***

Pippa made a slight detour on the way home and drove past the listed cottages. No van was parked there, Green Construction or otherwise. *Just passing through*, she thought, and tried not to feel smug. As far as she could tell, there were no notices on the lamp-posts either. Which meant no planning notices. Perhaps she would text Sheila later and let her know. Or perhaps it would keep until next Monday. Pippa sensed that her new babysitting arrangement was a little too fragile to withstand teasing.

Freddie talked to Ruby the whole way home, and Pippa turned the radio down so that she could listen to them.

'Did you have a nice time, Ruby? Did Granma give you treats?'

'Ga-ma?' Pippa imagined Ruby's round blue eyes and puzzled expression, and longed to look round and see if she was right.

'Yes, Granma. GRANMA.'

'Ga-ga.'

'Is that a yes?'

'Ga-ga.'

'One day you'll really talk, Ruby,' said Freddie, in a resigned tone.

'Ya.'

Lunch for Ruby was cheesy tomatoey pasta stars, which were unaccountably erratic in the way they jumped off the spoon whenever it got close to Ruby's gaping mouth. Freddie helped Pippa to scoop them off the tray of the highchair and attempt re-entry into Ruby's digestive system. 'Was I this messy, Mummy?'

'If anything you were worse, Freddie. Ruby's got you to set a good example.'

Freddie giggled, and his face showed a mixture of responsibility and mischief. Pippa wondered what she might have unleashed, then shelved the thought for later. There was pudding to get through yet.

Eventually Ruby was fed, cleaned, changed and put down for a nap. Pippa allowed Freddie half an hour of *SuperMouse* and went to make herself a sandwich. The kitchen clock said 1.45. *Once*, she thought, *mealtimes didn't take half a day*. For some reason, horrible school dinners came into her head. Cheese pie and salad with half a hard-boiled egg which had a black rim round the yolk. Custard with a skin on top. Strings of unidentifiable green veg which were either raw or mushy.

School dinners.

School . . . *admissions*.

Pippa cut her ham sandwich in half and took it to the

dining room. Peering at the picture on her phone, she entered the website address and watched the little circle spin, searching.

*Download School Admissions booklet (3 MB)*

Pippa clicked again.

The document opened while she was chewing. The cover depicted two children, hand in hand, dressed in a royal-blue school uniform. Pippa swallowed her bite of sandwich and it stuck in her throat. She fetched a glass of water to wash it down, but it remained, a hard unpleasant lump.

She began to scroll.

*You may choose three primary schools, and list them in order of preference on your application.*

Pippa blinked. The two primary schools she had heard of were the one in Much Gadding, and the one in Lower Gadding, three miles away. And the only reason she had heard of the second one was because Lila had mentioned it in passing.

*You must submit your application, either online or by post, by 15 January 2018. Failure to do so will mean that your child will be allocated a place at the nearest available school —*

Pippa relaxed.

*— which has vacancies.*

Pippa imagined waving Freddie off at the train station to a school on the other side of Gadcestershire, probably behind a mountain range guarded by sabre-toothed tigers.

*You can read about primary schools in Gadcestershire on the following pages…*

Pippa's index finger stroked the trackpad.

*St Andrew's...*

*St Asaph's...*

*St Cuthbert...*

*St David...*

How many saints were there? Pippa kept scrolling until she came to a heading in bold type: *Community Primary Schools*. But there were still pages and pages left to read; she could tell by the position of the scroll bar. And most of the schools were in places she had never visited. In desperation Pippa scrolled to *M. There. Start with what you know.*

*Much Gadding Primary School.*

*Age range: 4-11.*

*Pupil number: 30.*

*Pupils on roll: 196.*

*Was the school oversubscribed? Yes*

Pippa shivered.

*Ofsted rating: Good (2015)*

Was that good? She supposed it must be. Pippa's eyes flicked through the admissions criteria. The only one which applied to Freddie was distance from the school, measured in a straight line.

*Who walks anywhere in a straight line?* Pippa had a flashback to her own time at primary school, measuring the length of the playground using a wheel on a stick which clicked every time it passed a metre. She had wondered what the point was at the time, and maybe now she had the answer. If she had listened to her teacher, Miss Jennings, she could be sitting pretty in a cushy job as a school distance measurer.

*What I need is a map.* Pippa scrolled to the beginning of the document, and, what do you know, someone had anticipated her need on page 29. There was Gadcestershire in all its roughly diamond-shaped glory, with a large helping of red and blue squares sprinkled over Gadcester and the surrounding areas, and random dots everywhere else.

Pippa enlarged the map and peered. There were five dots within a five-mile range of Much Gadding: Much Gadding Primary, Lower Gadding Primary, St Patrick's Primary (Catholic) in Gadding Magna, Upper Gadding CE Primary, and an academy called Gadding Heights in Greater Gadding.

She sighed, reopened her notebook, and started a new page.

*School Info.*

'Muuuuuum!' Freddie called from the sitting room. '*SuperMouse* is finished, can we go and have fun now?'

Pippa closed the notebook and eyed her sandwich, which was missing precisely one bite. 'Just let me finish my lunch, Freddie, and when Ruby's awake that's exactly what we'll do.' She bit into her slightly firm sandwich. *Your whole future can wait till this evening, I suppose.*

# CHAPTER 3

'So what about this gig you mentioned for Jeff?' Lila asked while they were queuing for drinks at playgroup. 'Have you got dates for me?'

'Not yet,' said Pippa. 'I've been a bit — diverted.'

Lila's eyebrows shot into her curls. 'Pippa Parker, organiser and entrepreneur, *diverted?* What's brought this on?'

'School stuff,' said Pippa, feeling her whole body droop as she said the words.

'Oh, school stuff.' Lila waved a hand. 'Now we're free of Barbara's evil spell —'

'Ooh, that's a bit harsh,' said Eva, from behind them. 'Speak nothing but good of the dead, you know.'

'Are you worried she'll come back and haunt you?' Lila laughed. 'Come on, you know she had Shelley whatsits in her pocket —'

'Jackson,' Pippa said, automatically. 'Mrs Shelley Jackson.'

'Ooh dear, you have got a bad case, haven't you?' Lila remarked.

'Of what, clever clogs?'

'Informationitis. Been swotting up, have we?'

'And you haven't, of course.'

Lila grinned. 'I'm picking the three nearest, in order, and that'll have to do. Let's face it, most of the other schools in Gadcestershire are so far off there's no point considering them. Not even if the kids' loos are gold-plated and they'll leave knowing five languages and calculus.'

'I s'pose,' said Pippa, feeling slightly better. 'So you've looked at the map then.'

'Yup,' said Lila. 'I'll go to a few open days to check they don't do sacrifices or whippings, and then I'm good.'

'That's a bit casual, isn't it?' said Sam, as the queue shuffled forward. 'I mean, the school they go to will have a big influence on them.' She spoke hesitantly, as if she still expected to be shown the door at any moment. 'The local primary's only got a good rating. Some schools are outstanding.'

'And miles away,' said Lila. 'I don't want a long school run every day, I've got enough to do.' A warlike glint came into her eye. 'Before you say that's selfish, Sam, which I can see you're itching to do, I want Bella to have local school-friends and go to a feeder school for GadMag High, which as you no doubt know *is* rated as outstanding.'

Sam muttered something and studied the floor, and Pippa gave Lila a look which she hoped conveyed the message *you've won, now shut up*.

'What'll it be, ladies?' said Imogen, waving her hands at the pale-blue cups and saucers. 'Tea, coffee, squash? We have a range of biscuits and also mini cupcakes.'

'Cupcake and coffee, please,' said Pippa and Lila, simultaneously.

'How's the school hunt going?' asked Imogen, as she poured out.

'Don't go there,' said Pippa.

'I *know*,' Imogen replied. 'I mean, it would be easy if Much Gadding was two-form entry.'

Pippa goggled. 'Excuse me?'

'Sorry, jargon,' said Imogen. 'They're one-form entry so they have thirty places. If they were two-form, they'd take sixty. Plus once you look at all the kids with older siblings there, who get priority, half the places have already gone.' She shrugged and placed a cupcake on each saucer. 'There you go.'

'I never even *thought* of that,' Pippa whispered, as they weaved through the islands of busy toddlers and back to their chairs. 'What are we going to do?'

'Stay calm,' said Lila, sitting down. 'And stop that, Pippa.'

'Stop what?'

'Counting how many kids of Freddie's age there are in the room.'

'Was it that obvious?'

'*Yes*.' Lila grinned. 'When do you think you could let me know about that gig?'

'Soon,' said Pippa. 'Could Short Back and Sides do a whole concert?'

Lila snorted. 'Course they could.'

'They won't get sore throats or lose their voices?'

'*No*. They're professionals, Pip.'

'I was only asking.' Pippa heaved a sigh. 'Lady H wants a series of concerts at Higginbotham Hall, and I'm not entirely sure how I'm going to fill the slots. I mean, if Sweet Harmony are typical, we don't have enough songs in our repertoire for a whole concert. We could maybe do an hour.'

'Jeff and the gang probably have enough material for the whole lot,' said Lila, but the tone of her voice made Pippa look at her.

'Everything all right?' she muttered.

It was Lila's turn to sigh. 'Nothing's wrong.'

Pippa glanced at Ruby, who was crawling towards the play kitchen with great purpose. 'Eva,' she said, touching her neighbour's arm, 'would you mind watching Ruby for a couple of minutes? I'll just be in the kitchen.'

'Sure,' said Eva. 'If she escapes, I'll text.'

'Thanks.' Pippa got up, and after a pause Lila did too.

The kitchen was still occupied — Imogen was starting the washing up — so they hovered in the little corridor. 'So what's up?' asked Pippa.

Lila bit her lip. 'Nothing's up, exactly. I suppose that's the problem.'

'When you say nothing's up —'

'Not that!' Lila exclaimed, grinning. 'That is most definitely *not* the problem.'

'Oh, um, good —'

'Everything in *that* department is absolutely fine —'

'OK, OK, I get it!' Pippa held her hands up. 'Spare me the details, if you don't mind.'

'I will,' said Lila, with a cheeky smile. Then it vanished as if a cloud had blotted out the sun. 'But we aren't moving forward at all.'

'Ohh.'

'I mean, we're together most weekends, and I see Jeff when he's not doing choir stuff.' Lila looked uncomfortable, and Pippa sensed there was more to come.

'But…'

'But he hasn't said anything about moving in together, or — anything.'

'That's one too many anythings.'

'I know. But I'm not saying — that word.'

'The M word?'

'*No*.'

Pippa considered. 'You could ask him to move in, you know.'

'I could.' Lila was gazing at the toes of her sneakers. 'But I want him to ask me to — God knows why, after last time, but I do.'

'You sound about fourteen.'

'I know. You'd be exactly the same.'

Pippa smiled. 'Yes, I probably would.'

'It's all right for you,' Lila said, and her voice had an edge. 'You and Simon have been married for ever.'

'No we haven't!'

'Well, ever since I've known you, which comes to the same thing.' Lila glanced at the door to the main hall. 'How long *have* you been married?'

Pippa thought. *Darn, I ought to know this off the top of my head.* 'We got married in 2013.'

'So not that long before Freddie, then?'

'No. Freddie was a honeymoon baby. Probably.' Pippa grinned.

'But you went out for ages before that, right?'

'Nooooo, a couple of years.'

'Really?' Lila looked shocked. 'I always assumed you were childhood sweethearts.'

'Good grief, no. We met at a gig in a pub. Suze's then-boyfriend was managing a band, so she dragged me along, and Simon was a friend of the bassist. Or was it the drummer?' Pippa frowned as she tried to remember. 'The friend was definitely called John, whatever his instrument was.'

'Now that sounds cool. Much better than picking up a man at the bank,' Lila said, regretfully.

'More convenient, though. And steady.'

'I thought once we'd decided we liked each other Jeff would be all let's-settle-down. But he's so busy with Short Back and Sides that I sometimes think he's going steady with them, not me.'

'How long have you been going out, though? Six months?'

'More like nine,' Lila shot back.

'Yes, but not that long. Maybe he wants to take things slowly.'

'He might,' Lila's mouth drooped. 'Bella's already asked me if she can be my bridesmaid.'

'Oh God! What did you say?'

'What could I say?' Lila studied the floor again. 'I said we hadn't arranged anything yet and she asked if we weren't getting married.' She looked up, and her eyes blazed. 'It's all right for *him*, he doesn't have to deal with this!'

'That's hardly his fault,' Pippa pointed out, feeling disloyal.

Lila softened immediately. 'I know.' She seemed to be turning something over in her mind. 'Would Simon have a word with him? Maybe take him for a pint?'

Pippa's eyes widened. 'Simon?'

'Yeah, you know, that bloke you're married to. Jeff might open up to him.'

'But they don't really know each other.'

'Well maybe they should. If — you know.'

'I'll ask him. I'm not saying yes for him, though.'

'Jeff's good company when you get to know him.' Lila sounded put out. 'He could do a Monday or a Wednesday, or maybe a Sunday.'

'A school night?'

'There isn't much else left. Choir practice, and stuff.' Lila spoke briskly, but a hint of sadness lurked underneath which made Pippa want to hug her, although she knew it would be exactly the wrong thing to do. Unless she actually wanted Lila to have a crying fit outside the kitchen.

'I'll see what I can do.' She touched Lila's arm as a compromise.

Lila's mouth trembled for a moment, then she smiled. 'You're a star, Pip. Thanks.' She detached herself from the wall. 'Come on, let's see what the rugrats have been doing.'

Ruby was hitting the play saucepans with a wooden spoon, while Bella had joined Freddie and Henry in a game they called 'Garage Slam', whose rules were far too complex — or perhaps badly explained — for any grown-up to fathom. 'Quiet as a little mouse,' Eva said, above the din.

'Thanks for minding her,' said Pippa.

'No probs,' Eva replied. She leaned closer and lowered her voice. 'Were you talking about school stuff?'

'No, something else,' said Pippa. 'Are you looking this year?'

Eva nodded. 'We want her to go to St Patrick's, but after that the nearest Catholic school is in Gadcester.' Her face was dejected. 'We might put Much Gadding as our first choice, as we're so close.'

'Oh yes, so you are.' Eva lived in one of the little modern houses along the road from the school. 'It does make sense.' In her head Pippa saw a marble rolling down a chute and dropping into one of fifteen hollows. *Filled.*

***

'You want me to what?' said Simon, spearing a meatball with his fork and dispatching half. The other half fell off his fork and plopped into his spaghetti.

'Erm, go for a pint with Jeff and sound him out?'

'About what?' His tone was abrupt, and Pippa wished she'd waited for a better time. But there was no going back now.

'His, um, intentions.'

'They've only been seeing each other for two minutes. Does he have to have intentions?' Simon captured the errant meatball and chewed, winding more spaghetti on his fork as he did so. 'You do realise, Pip, that to ask Jeff out for a pint I need his phone number. I don't have it, and I don't think you do either because you always arrange things through Lila. Jeff'll work out it's some sort of set-up, and if he does agree we'll spend an evening making awkward conversation, then say we should do it again sometime and leave it there. So no, I don't think it's a good idea.'

'OK, you've got a point.' Pippa sighed. 'Lila seemed so down, though. I just wanted to help.'

'I know.' Simon put his fork down and reached for her hand. 'And it's sweet of you. But I don't think I *can* help.'

'Fair enough. I'll let her know.' Pippa concentrated on getting spaghetti onto her own fork. 'How was work, anyway?'

'The usual. In-house meetings back to back with supplier teleconferences.'

'I can't tell if that's good or bad.'

'It's business. Oh, and I've got a bit of news for you. Guess who I saw in the village?'

'No idea. Who?'

'Tony Green.'

Pippa racked her brains for a friend or work colleague, past or present, called Tony, and came up blank. 'Should I know him?'

'He's Green Construction, you know, the eco-friendly building firm. Carbon-neutral developments and all that.'

'And you saw him at work?'

'God, no. I popped into the bakery on the way home for a wholemeal sliced, like you asked me to, and there he was chatting up Pam like he'd never left.'

'So he's local?'

'Was local. Tony was a couple of years above me at GadMag, and he was an eco warrior even then. Although some of that involved not bothering with deodorant or shampoo. Stinky Green, his nickname was. Though he seems to have got over that.'

'Maybe he's visiting family.'

'Don't think so. He left GadMag after GCSEs and I'm sure I heard they moved up to York. Plus he's staying at the bed and breakfast next door to the bakery. He said so.'

'Nostalgia trip, maybe.'

Simon shrugged. 'Maybe.' He carried on eating his spaghetti. 'I wonder if he's here for a reason.'

Pippa twirled her fork, but her heart wasn't in it. A Green Construction van yesterday, and the man himself today, being nice to shopkeepers. Whatever Tony Green's personal habits these days, she definitely smelt a rat.

# CHAPTER 4

The phone rang two minutes after Pippa had pressed *Send* on her text to Sheila. Pippa hurried into the hall, wishing Sheila wouldn't default to the landline, and picked it up.

'I *knew* that van meant something,' Sheila said, her voice full of righteous glee.

'Maybe you were right,' said Pippa.

There was a significant pause at Sheila's end, and Pippa wondered what might be coming next. She had a distinct feeling Sheila hadn't phoned to request more babysitting opportunities, or ask for her scone recipe.

'So,' said Sheila, 'what do we do now?'

'We?'

'Yes, we.'

'About what?'

'Whatever Mr Green Construction is planning for the meadow.'

'Um, I suppose we wait and see if a planning application goes in. They usually put notices up at the site when they do.'

'That isn't very proactive,' Sheila scolded. 'You should be sniffing around for information.'

'I'm not a bloodhound. And there may not be any information. For all we know it could be just an idea. Or maybe Tony Green is here for a break.'

'I can tell you don't believe that, Pippa.'

'Maybe not. But I'm too busy with work and trying to choose a school for Freddie to want more things to chase after.'

'A school for Freddie?' Sheila's voice was sharp. Pippa wasn't sure whether to congratulate herself on a successful diversion tactic or wish she hadn't started a new hare. 'That can't be yet. Surely he'll just go to Much Gadding like the boys did.'

'It is yet. And he might not get into Much Gadding. It's all about siblings and distance.'

'Oh.' Sheila's sigh was audible down the phone. 'Now if Barbara were still alive, it wouldn't be a problem. She'd have a word in the right place and Bob's your uncle.'

'Is that fair?'

'Does it matter, if you get the right result?' Sheila's voice was clipped, matter-of-fact. 'It's a dog-eat-dog world, Pippa. You know a lot of people, and I'm sure you wouldn't have any difficulty getting Freddie in, *if you chose to*. And you could probably get the inside scoop on any planning decisions, *if you wanted*.'

'Well I don't want.' Pippa felt herself growing warm. 'I'd better go, Sheila, Ruby will probably wake soon —'

'Just one more thing,' said Sheila. 'Which is closer to

the primary school, your house or the meadow?'

'The meadow, of course.'

'Exactly. Goodnight dear,' said Sheila, and put the phone down.

Pippa replaced the phone on its cradle, and found herself staring at it. She blinked and went through to the sitting room, where Simon was watching the news. 'Lila OK?' he asked, without turning his head.

'That wasn't Lila, that was your mother.'

Now he turned. 'What did she want?'

'I texted that you'd seen Tony Green in the village.'

Simon looked blank.

'Sheila saw a Greens van parked by the meadow yesterday morning.'

He snorted. 'And you two suspect there is skulduggery afoot.'

'She does.' Pippa sat opposite him. 'If they are building on the meadow it might affect Freddie's schooling.'

Simon grabbed the remote from the coffee table and switched the TV off. '*What?*'

'If they build houses on it, those will be nearer the primary —'

'Is that how they decide primary-school places? How do you know?'

'It's in the booklet.'

'What booklet?' Simon demanded, his eyebrows lowering.

'The school admissions booklet.'

'How come I don't know about this?'

'I just found out myself!' cried Pippa. 'There was a

poster on the preschool door. I only downloaded it yesterday.'

'Oh.' Simon sat back a little. 'I didn't realise.' Then he leaned forward. 'You could have told me though.'

'I meant to, but I spent most of the day organising the concerts for Lady H, and then Ruby was grizzly in the evening, so I forgot.'

Simon frowned again.

'We've got till January, you know.'

'Well I wouldn't know, would I?' But his voice was reasonable rather than combative. 'Come on, let's make a brew and look at it together.'

***

An hour later, they weren't much further on.

'I'd rather Freddie made his own mind up about religion,' said Pippa.

'That's all very well, but if he can't get into my old school I want him to go somewhere outstanding.'

'But we don't go to church.'

'I was christened; that must count for something. I bet Mum's got a picture tucked away, or a baptism certificate, or whatever you get as evidence.'

'See, it's so important to you that you don't even know what it is.'

Simon glared at her, and Pippa had to admit that she probably deserved it. Then he sat back. 'Of course there's always private school. That would bypass the whole problem.'

'But —'

'But what? It's an option,' Simon said, very reasonably.

Pippa imagined Freddie in a blazer and a straw boater, punting a tiny boat down the River Gad, then shook the picture out of her head. 'I don't like the idea of it.'

'Well, maybe we should look at some — and the prices — and see what we think.'

'Mmm.'

'Let's sleep on it.' Simon closed the lid of the laptop. 'We aren't getting anywhere, and we'll just end up arguing.'

Pippa sighed. 'Yes.' She looked at the laptop. Really she ought to be doing more research for Lady Higginbotham's concerts, or checking booking numbers for Serendipity's craft demonstration tour, which now seemed to take in every church hall this side of Gadcester, but Sheila, schools and Simon had sapped all her energy. And as if on cue, an electronic wail from the baby alarm signalled that Ruby required attention.

***

The child on the school admissions poster had a slightly more reproachful look on her face the next morning when Pippa dropped Freddie off. She blinked, and rang the bell.

'Hello, Mrs Parker,' said Mrs Marks, as she opened it. 'Ah, and here's Ruby back from her adventures.' She leaned down to Ruby, who clapped her dimpled hands.

'Indeed she is,' said Pippa. 'In you go, Freddie. There's Livvy.'

Livvy looked up at the sound of her name, then smiled shyly at Freddie, who shouted 'Hello Livvy' although she was perhaps five feet away.

'It's shepherd's pie with carrots today,' said Mrs Marks.

‘Back at the usual time?’

‘Well, yes,’ said Pippa, feeling slightly got at.

‘Jolly good,’ said Mrs Marks heartily. ‘See you then.’

Pippa wheeled Ruby away. ‘Let’s go for a walk, shall we? Maybe we can feed the ducks.’

‘Dak dak!’ said Ruby, which Pippa took as assent. Yet somehow Pippa found herself wheeling the pushchair past the village green and the duck pond, and crossing just at the point where the footpath to the meadow began. As Pippa reached the pavement her attention was diverted by a new poster on the board, with a large heading in letters made out of green leaves: *PUBLIC CONSULTATION*.

Pippa wheeled Ruby closer to read the rest of the notice.

*Dear residents of Much Gadding,*

*You are all invited to an open public consultation event, to take place on Thursday 21st September, 7-8.30pm, at St Saviour’s Church Hall (it was the biggest place in the village we could book).*

*The purpose of the consultation is to seek your views on future use of the land behind the cottages on Gadding Lane (next to Polly’s Whatnots).*

*We at Green Construction would like to investigate the possibility of providing affordable green housing as part of this space, and we would love to know what you think. Please come and share your ideas.*

*Yours sincerely,*

*Tony Green*

*Founder of Green Construction*

In her head Pippa heard the words 'I *knew* it,' in Sheila's voice. She took a picture of the notice with her phone, sent it to Simon, Sheila, and Lila, then walked into the village. She had promised Ruby ducks, and ducks she would supply.

However, both the resident ducks of the pond were asleep on the bank, heads under their wings, as if they had had a rough night. Pippa sat on the bench and gave Ruby a rice cake, but her heart wasn't in it.

Ruby mumbled on her snack for a couple of minutes, then said 'Da!' triumphantly and threw it on the ground. 'Come on, you,' said Pippa, eyeing the clouds gathering overhead. 'Let's go to the library.'

On the way round the green Pippa saw more posters; one in the grocer's window, one on the door of the Cross Keys, and one pinned on the newspaper board at the county store. The library had one too, and Pippa half-expected to find a gaggle of angry residents inside, holding forth about green belt and conservation areas. When she pushed the door open, though, the library was as quiet as ever.

The newspaper at the end of the room lowered, and Norm peered round it cautiously. Relief crossed his face, and he put the paper on the desk, still open. 'Hello, Pippa.'

'Hi, Norm.' Pippa wheeled Ruby over. 'Were you expecting someone else?'

'I'm not sure what to expect,' said Norm, ruefully. 'I've had all sorts in this morning trying to pump me for information.'

'That's good, isn't it? The quest for knowledge, and

all that.'

'Not when it's about a consultation and I know less than they do.'

'The one for the meadow? I've seen the posters.'

'As has most of Much Gadding.' Norm wrinkled his nose. 'Because Susan's a parish councillor, they think I have insider information. Which I don't.'

'Oh.'

'Yes, and several people refuse to believe me.' Norm had an indefinable bristliness about him, far from his usual easygoing attitude. 'I'll be glad when it's out in the open, whatever it is.' A shadow crossed his face. 'You haven't come in for the same thing, have you?'

'No!' said Pippa. 'I was — well — at a loose end.'

Norm exhaled. 'Take your time.'

Pippa wheeled Ruby to the children's section and found some board books to read to her. Ruby's legs thumped against the pushchair as Pippa read and showed her the pictures, though her comments, 'Da!', 'Ba!', and 'Wa!', didn't have much relation to what she was seeing. Pippa gave Ruby her buggy activity toy, a device with mirrors, rattles, and bits to pull on which she supposed was a sort of Swiss Army Knife for babies, and parked her by the crime section. Yet nothing seemed right. The Golden Age was too decorous, and the thrillers too violent. She just felt sad and uncertain. In the end she chose two books which she'd seen lots of publicity for, and took them to the counter.

Norm raised his eyebrows. 'Not your usual selections, Pippa.'

'I know. I'm not sure what I feel like.'

He wrote the books down in his ledger, then looked up. 'Everything all right?'

Pippa shrugged, and Ruby squealed loud enough to make them both wince. 'I'll take madam away,' said Pippa. 'She hasn't grasped yet that libraries are usually quiet.'

'Good to see you,' said Norm, and pulled the newspaper towards him.

Pippa checked her watch as she left the library. Eleven o'clock. There was really no alternative but to head home and do something either financially or domestically useful. But her steps dragged. What did Tony Green have in mind for the meadow, and would it affect Freddie and Ruby's future? And not just theirs, but potentially the children of all her local friends? She swallowed the thought and strode briskly towards home. A good session of cleaning might push it out of her head.

# CHAPTER 5

When Pippa, Simon and the children arrived at the church hall a queue was already snaking back to the pavement, and it was only a quarter to seven. 'Quite a turnout,' Simon observed.

Marge whipped round, glaring. Her expression softened as she saw who it was. 'Come to add your voice to the throng?' she asked.

'We've come to hear what Tony Green's got to say,' he responded. 'I'm not making my mind up till then.'

'If you *can* hear,' said Marge. 'The door's already open, you know. We're overspill.'

Pippa looked round. People were still arriving. Some appeared faintly curious, as if they were about to try a much-hyped new food, but many wore an expression suggesting they had either a bone to pick or an axe to grind, and they were waiting to find out which of the two it was.

'Excuse me, everyone,' called a voice from the hall, and

a tallish, slim man appeared in the doorway, dressed in jeans and a green T-shirt. His brown hair reached almost to his shoulders, and he had a neat, trimmed beard. He looked rather like a conventional picture of Jesus, only without the halo.

'The man himself,' muttered Simon.

*So this is Tony Green*, thought Pippa. On balance, she wasn't surprised.

'The hall's full already, and I can see there are quite a few more of you. As we won't be able to get you all in, I propose we head over to the village green. It isn't far, and it's a fine night. I didn't expect so many people!' He grinned, and Pippa found herself liking him. 'I'll just collect the pictures, then I'll lead the way over.' He vanished, and a buzz of conversation filled the space where he had been.

'He's young, isn't he?'

'Do you think he's in charge?'

'I'm not being taken in by some softly-softly approach.'

'I wonder if he's married…'

'I bet he's a vegetarian. Or maybe even a vegan. He's got that air about him.'

Eventually Tony Green re-emerged with a large roll of paper under his arm, followed by two men, also in green T-shirts, each carrying a folded-down trestle table. 'Let's go!' he said, and the sizeable crowd trailed in his wake down the road to the green. From the snatches of conversation around her, some people were mollified by the unexpected move, while others saw it as a delaying tactic which clearly meant this Green man was up to no good.

Tony Green strolled to a bench and hopped onto it, holding his arms out to the sides for a moment as if getting his balance on a surfboard. 'Sorry to loom over you like this, but I think it's the only way you'll all be able to see and hear me,' he said, his voice slightly raised.

More people were coming now; some looked irritated, perhaps not pleased at being caught out. Pippa glimpsed Beryl Harbottle, stern-faced, and behind her was Lady Higginbotham. Pippa was surprised to see that her expression was stern too. She didn't think Lady Higginbotham had it in her.

'Here you are,' said a cross voice, and Sheila tapped her on the shoulder. 'You could have said they'd changed the venue.'

'It just happened,' said Pippa defensively.

'Oh, hi Mum,' said Simon. 'You remember Tony Green?'

'No, not really,' said Sheila.

The grass of the green was barely visible for people. Pippa felt a nudge, and Lila grinned at her. 'We can always attack him if we don't like his plan,' she said conversationally. 'Burn him at the stake or whatnot. I'm sure there's enough people here to count as an angry mob.'

'A slightly affronted mob, really,' said Jeff behind her, holding Bella's hand.

'Hi, Jeff,' said Pippa. 'I didn't think you'd be interested in a Much Gadding matter.' Jeff lived over in Greater Gadding, in what Lila described as an obsessively-neat bachelor pad.

'Well, you never know,' he said, and studied the row

of shops.

Lila nudged Pippa again, and Pippa made a *yes-I-heard* face. Lila cast a sidelong glance at Simon.

'Everyone,' called Tony Green, his voice a little thin in the cool September air. 'Thank you for coming. I'll try and keep it brief as you're standing; this isn't exactly how I imagined it.'

A few giggles from the crowd, and a couple of wisecracks.

'I grew up in Much Gadding, until my family moved north when I was sixteen.'

A faint rumble from the crowd, which might have been surprise or approval.

'I've always had an interest in ecology, in making the most of our green spaces, and enjoying them while helping them to flourish. And I'm aware that there is a housing shortage in Much Gadding. Lots of people who would like to live here can't.'

The rumble rose, and seemed to sour a little.

'Without more houses and places to live, perhaps our children won't be able to make their homes in Much Gadding. Or the surrounding areas.'

The rumble paused, and Tony went on. He spoke of sustainable, carbon-neutral living, of solar panels and sedum roofs and rainwater collection. His voice rose and fell as he made sweeping gestures with his arms, and he seemed perfectly at home standing on his bench, preaching the good life. Pippa let the words wash over her, and her eyes closed…

A tug on her sleeve. 'Mummy,' whispered Freddie,

'will he stop talking soon?'

'I don't know,' Pippa whispered back. 'Maybe a few more minutes.'

'Oh.' Freddie was shifting from foot to foot. 'I, um…'

'Do you need a wee?'

He nodded enthusiastically and stifled a yawn.

'OK,' said Pippa, looking at her watch. 'It's past your bedtime anyway. Come on, I'll take you and Ruby home.' Ruby's eyes were drooping too. Hopefully Pippa could get her home and into bed before she fell fast asleep.

Pippa excuse-med her way through the crowd, which moved aside grudgingly, and walked home, Freddie half-running at her side. '*Quickly*, Mummy!' He dashed into the house and ran to the downstairs toilet.

'So much for getting the full story,' she told Ruby, unbuckling her and lifting her out. 'Oh dear, it smells like you needed to go too.' The words *Stinky Green* came into her head and she snorted, then reproved herself. Of course teenagers went through phases of not washing and stuff like that; it was a normal part of growing up. And while Tony Green's hair might be a bit long, it — and he — looked presentable enough.

***

'I didn't think you'd be out that long,' she said, when Simon got home. 'Was there a big fight?'

'A heated debate, really,' said Simon, throwing his keys on the hall table and coming into the lounge, where Pippa was treating herself to a gin and tonic. 'The naturalists were a bit hot under the collar, but Tony knew his stuff about protected species so that took the wind out of their sails. Then the archaeologists weighed in, but Tony said he'd fund a preliminary dig, and explained that there were no active restrictions to building on the meadow. And he's already in talks with the council about buying the land subject to planning permission.'

'So he came prepared.'

'He certainly did.'

'What about the not-in-my-backyard types?'

Simon considered. 'They were a bit quiet, actually. I think Tony's vision of a better Much Gadding for all made them a bit shy about speaking up.'

'Sounds like a fun evening.' Pippa took a large sip of her drink.

'Did the kids go down OK?'

'Oh, fine. Freddie was knackered, he was asleep almost before I'd left the room.'

'He did look tired.' Simon leaned down and kissed her.

'Wait a minute,' Pippa said, suspiciously. 'You taste of beer. Have you had a sneaky pint?'

'I have indeed,' said Simon smugly. 'And you can't tell me off because I had a pint with Jeff, so I was following orders.' He sat beside Pippa.

Pippa twisted round to stare at him. 'You had a drink with Jeff? What brought this on?'

Simon grinned. 'I frogmarched him to the Fiddler. Not really. Lila took Bella home maybe fifteen minutes after you left, and Jeff stayed put with me so that we could dish any dirt to you both later. I mean report developments. So when the meeting broke up at twenty to nine, a pint seemed in order.'

‘And how did you get on?’

‘He’s OK, actually. I thought he might be a bit, um, theatrical, but we had a good chat.’

‘What about?’

‘Stuff,’ said Simon.

‘Lila stuff?’

‘Stuff,’ Simon repeated, firmly.

‘Not fair,’ said Pippa, feeling injured. ‘You two don’t get to be best buddies and gang up on us.’

‘No-one’s ganging up on anyone,’ said Simon, leaning back against the sofa. ‘Unless it’s Tony Green.’ He paused. ‘The proposed housing looked nice. Cedar-clad cabin-style stuff. A bit like a holiday let.’ Then his mouth twitched. ‘But if it messes with Freddie’s primary-school place at Much Gadding, I’m opposing it.’

‘Mmm,’ said Pippa, and finished her drink. She didn’t feel much more informed than she had before the meeting. But if Tony Green had an answer to everything, she didn’t see how the new housing could be opposed. She imagined herself at Gadcester station, waving a handkerchief as Freddie flourished his straw boater from the departing train.

***

‘How did you get on with the books?’ Norm asked, when Pippa put them on the counter the next morning.

‘I didn’t,’ said Pippa. ‘I gave the first one fifty pages but I didn’t even get that far, and I found two spelling mistakes in the first chapter of the other one.’

‘Oh,’ said Norm. ‘Well, you tried something new. It doesn’t always work.’

‘Back to the crime shelves…’ Pippa heard a *ping* and automatically reached for her phone. But her screen was blank.

Norm grunted and brought a small blue phone out of his pocket. ‘Oh,’ he said, his face falling. ‘I thought so.’

‘Is everything all right?’ asked Pippa. ‘If you have to go somewhere I could mind the library for you. Until I need to get Freddie, anyway.’

‘No, no,’ said Norm absently. ‘It’s just —’ He looked up. ‘That was a text from Susan. She’s had an email about a new planning application. From Green Construction.’

# CHAPTER 6

Tony Green might as well have pulled the pin from a grenade and tossed it onto the village green. The Much Gadding Naturalists Society, led by Terry Ransome (a man who rather resembled an affronted heron), hung a sheet painted with the slogan *Save Our Green Space* at the entrance to the meadow, until the woman who lived in the cottage next door complained that it was an eyesore. Pippa now knew that Malcolm, the mild-looking elderly man she saw in the library occasionally, was Malcolm Allason, president of the Much Gadding Archaeological Society; the local free newsletter and the *Messenger* had featured several articles of his, lamenting the desecration of a meadow of historical importance.

Everyone had an opinion, it seemed. Lila, Marge, Serendipity and Caitlin were in favour of the new houses. 'Let's face it,' said Lila, 'no-one goes to the meadow. I'd forgotten it was there till this kicked off. So maybe putting a few more affordable houses on it is a good move.

Especially if it means more people can stay in the village.' Her eyes shone.

'Thinking of moving?' asked Pippa, teasingly.

'Oh shut up,' Lila snapped. Then she relaxed. 'If Jeff and I ever did get somewhere together…'

'Ah.' Lila threw a cushion at Pippa, who ducked.

Marge was more practical. 'I'm not getting any younger, and neither is Wisteria Cottage. If young Tony Green can show me somewhere cheaper and easier to run, I'm in.' She snorted. 'Although I'm not sure how Mr Eco-Man would feel about Beyoncé eating the wildlife.'

On the other side were Sheila, Sam, Imogen, and Simon. Sheila's main objection was that it would be a change.

'But if nothing in the village ever changed —' Pippa began.

'I like it as it is,' said Sheila, firmly.

Sam and Imogen were opposed to the development solely on the grounds that it might affect Livvy and Henry's places at Much Gadding. 'If it wasn't for that, I wouldn't care either way,' Imogen said at playgroup. 'But it might.'

'Exactly,' said Sam.

And Simon felt the same way. 'I thought you'd be in favour of new housing,' said Pippa, feeling a little bewildered as she watched him type. He was writing an email to the council to oppose the development. He had told her this before he opened the laptop, and she couldn't work out whether his purpose in doing so was to suggest she should do the same, or to convince himself that it was the right thing to do.

'Normally I would be,' said Simon. 'But not if it affects Freddie.'

'It might not,' said Pippa. 'Don't forget we're going on the school tour tomorrow.'

Simon looked over the laptop at her. 'You don't sound overjoyed.' There was a note of accusation in his voice.

'It isn't that,' said Pippa. 'It feels weird having to make a decision. I just hope we like it. It's our closest option.'

'Mmm,' said Simon, and returned to his email.

***

Freddie skipped ahead of Pippa and Ruby as they walked past the village green. 'We're going to see my school today, we're going to see my school today!' he sang. His excitement had been almost uncontrollable since breakfast. At least their visit was at ten in the morning. Freddie might have exploded if he had had to wait till the afternoon.

Out of habit Pippa turned in at the gate which led to preschool. 'Not that one, Mummy!' Freddie cried. 'The next one!' She could see other parents converging on the entrance; Eva was there, and Sam, and Imogen. Pippa wheeled Ruby to join the crowd, and nodded to her friends, but kept separate. She wanted to be able to take in all she could about the school without distraction.

'It's five to,' said a decisive voice, belonging to a woman Pippa didn't know. 'I'm going to ring the bell.' She rang, waited, and at a faint buzz, pushed the door open.

A woman in a jumper and knee-length skirt bustled round the reception desk to meet them, her name badge swinging. 'You're all here for the tour? Let me mark you off.' She reached for a clipboard on the desk and ticked through the names efficiently. 'Two more to come, good. I'll tell Mrs Jackson you've arrived.' She walked to the back of the entrance hall and tapped on a door with a metal plate: *Mrs S Jackson, Headteacher*. After a moment she opened it and Pippa caught a glimpse of trophies and shields in a corner cabinet before the receptionist filled the gap. A brief exchange, and she closed it. 'Mrs Jackson's just on the phone,' she said. 'She won't be a minute.' She resumed her seat. 'Do have a look at the display boards.'

Pippa did as she was told, admiring a set of collages on the theme of space. Marbled-paper planets and tinfoil spaceships frolicked in skies festooned with silver and sometimes gold stars. On a table stood some formidable aliens created from washing-up liquid bottles and pipe-cleaners, inhabiting a papier-mâché moon crater.

'Wow,' breathed Freddie. 'I want to do that!'

On the other wall were a set of bright drawings labelled *Picasso Class Portraits*. Pippa doubted that any of Class 3B really had both eyes on the same side of their nose, but everyone was smiling.

The receptionist rose. 'I'll remind Mrs Jackson that you're waiting.' A few people mumbled thanks. She tapped at the door again, and this time Pippa heard the scrape of a chair.

Mrs Jackson was a smallish, broad-shouldered woman, perhaps in her early to mid-fifties, wearing a navy suit and court shoes. 'Good morning, everyone,' she said, hands clasped before her. 'Sorry to keep you waiting. Welcome to

Much Gadding Primary. My name is Shelley Jackson, and I have been the headteacher here for fifteen years.'

Various murmurs of approval. One person seemed to be taking notes on her phone.

'We'll start in the hall. If I can ask you to keep together… You'll appreciate that this is a normal school day so we won't disturb the pupils at their lessons.' Mrs Jackson opened the door and held it for everyone to pass through. Pippa smiled at her as she went past, and noticed that the hand which held the door was gripping it very firmly.

Standing in the hall, Mrs Jackson pointed out the gym equipment, outlined the school's healthy eating and PE programmes, and emphasised the importance of whole-school assemblies. Sam raised a hand. 'If we can leave questions till the end,' said Mrs Jackson, without pausing. 'Generally whatever parents want to ask is covered somewhere in the tour, and we need to finish by break time.'

Sam lowered her hand, and rolled her eyes at Pippa.

The party were shown the weekly menu, then conducted into a small library where Mrs Jackson talked about the homework policy and emphasised that parents were expected to read with their child regularly and fill in a reading journal. Pippa felt her face burning. She sneaked a look at the others, and noted that most were studying the floor, with a couple of parents beaming as if they had done their homework three weeks early and got full marks.

Their next stop was an empty classroom. 'Class 4G are on a trip today,' said Mrs Jackson. She waited for everyone to get in and arrange themselves, and had just opened her mouth to speak when a tap sounded at the door. 'I'm sorry to disturb you, Mrs Jackson,' said the receptionist. 'Mr Lonsdale from the council is on the phone.'

'I do apologise,' said Mrs Jackson. 'I'll ask Miss Knight to take over, and return as soon as I can.' Her heels clicked away.

'Um, do have a look at the displays,' said the receptionist, fidgeting.

A couple of minutes later a petite woman with short blondish hair walked in. She wore black wide-legged trousers and a stripy top, and she had a smear of blue paint on her left forearm. 'I'm Mrs Jackson's stunt double,' she said, smiling. 'Emma Knight, deputy head. What would you like to know that hasn't come up yet?'

Various hands went up, and she laughed. 'You're a well-behaved class. OK, I'll go from left to right.' She pointed to Sam.

'I wanted to ask about school assemblies and religion,' said Sam, sounding nervous. 'How do you handle it?'

Emma Knight smiled. 'The first thing I should say is that I'm quite new to this school; I joined two years ago. Traditionally the school is broadly Christian in its religious education. However, we are working to introduce more study of different religions.'

'Thank you,' Sam murmured, looking as if she was being buffeted by a strong gale.

The next parent had a crafty expression on her face. 'I note that your last Ofsted report, three years ago, rated the school as good. What are you doing to try and increase that rating to outstanding?'

'This school has always had a strong record for achievement in literacy and numeracy —' She grinned. 'Reading and writing to you and me. Now we are integrating wider learning into the curriculum — more geography, history, languages and science. We also want to support our pupils better and promote leadership throughout the school. We have a buddy scheme for the children, and we are looking at ways to support each other as teachers and continue our develop —'

'Thank you for holding the fort, Miss Knight,' Mrs Jackson said briskly, from the doorway. 'I'll take it from here.'

'Of course, Mrs Jackson.' Miss Knight smiled at the assembled parents. 'It was nice to meet you all, and I hope I'll see you again soon.' Her flat rubber-soled shoes made no noise as she left.

'Now, where were we?' said Mrs Jackson, advancing into the room.

'Miss Knight was taking questions,' said Pippa.

'Ah,' said Mrs Jackson. 'Any more for me?'

Pippa hesitated, then decided to plunge in. 'I understand this school is popular, and that you get more applicants than you have places.'

Mrs Jackson preened slightly. 'We are a popular school, yes.'

'So might the school expand to two classes per year?'

'We are a village school,' said Mrs Jackson smoothly. 'I don't think Much Gadding has sufficient families to fill a school double this size. We would be pulling other children away from their home villages to come here. It would have to be a very large extension or a whole new build, and we would probably have to put it on our school playing field, which no-one would want. So it doesn't seem likely, especially in these tough economic times. Any more questions?'

The Ofsted parent enquired whether the school offered coaching for entrance exams, and was met with a no. 'If some teachers wish to offer this privately, though, that is their business,' said Mrs Jackson, with a look of faint distaste, before checking her watch. 'As morning break is a minute away, I'm afraid that that is the end of the tour. I hope you have found it useful, and as Miss Knight has said, I hope to see you next September. This way, please.' She led them to the entrance hall, where the receptionist ticked them off her list in reverse.

'Did you enjoy it?' she asked, breezily.

'Um, yes, I think so,' said Pippa.

'First one?'

Pippa nodded.

'Thought so. There's a lot to a school, you know. More than you realise until you're in the position of choosing one.' She grinned. 'Mine just went to the nearest — they're grown up now — and I can't say I'm sorry.'

'What do you think, Freddie?' Pippa asked, once they were outside.

A range of expressions passed across Freddie's face, like clouds on a windy day. 'I liked it,' he said, finally. 'But…' His face contorted again, as if trying to twist out what he wanted to say.

They walked on a little further.

'She didn't talk to us,' Freddie blurted out. 'Not to me or Livvy or Henry or any of the children. She just talked to the mums and dads.'

'Mrs Jackson?'

'The lady in blue. The one in trousers smiled at me, but the first one didn't.'

'I think she was busy,' said Pippa, though she stored the information away for future rumination. 'If we hurry, we can get to playgroup for snack time.'

Freddie brightened immediately. 'Come on, Mummy!' He pulled on Pippa's arm, and Ruby's pushchair skewed to the right.

'Steady on, Fred-Fred!' But Pippa was relieved to see him looking happier. She hadn't even thought about the effect the school selection process might have on Freddie, and she berated herself for being a careless mother. Although if she'd got someone to mind Freddie, and hadn't involved him, that would have been wrong too… If Sam and Imogen came to playgroup, maybe they could chew it over while the children played…

'Look, Mummy,' said Freddie, pointing. 'What's he running for?'

A man had galloped across the road, narrowly avoiding a passing car, and was running towards them. Pippa recognised Malcolm Allason, but on his face was an expression of shock, mingled with something like awe.

'Are you all right?' she asked, stepping into his path. She knew him to speak to, just about.

He seemed to see her, and the pushchair, for the first

time. 'Me? I'm — I'm,' he panted. 'I found — on the meadow — I must tell someone.'

Pippa frowned. Surely an axe head or a random fossil wouldn't provoke this sort of reaction? Had he found buried treasure? 'I didn't know you were digging.'

'Not digging. No need to dig.' He made an odd noise as he rubbed his right eye, and Pippa saw that he was crying. 'A body, in the long grass. *A dead body,'* he mouthed. 'And I think it's Tony Green.'

# CHAPTER 7

Pippa stared at Malcolm. 'You're sure?' she said, eventually.

He nodded, gulping.

Pippa rummaged for her phone. 'I'll call an ambulance. Can you go back and stay with —'

Malcolm shook his head. 'I don't want —'

'Malcolm, I *can't.*' Pippa pointed at Freddie in what she hoped was a discreet manner. 'Just — go and keep people away.' Malcolm's gaze dropped and he walked slowly over the road.

'What's happened, Mummy?' asked Freddie, touching her hand.

'I think someone's had an accident, Freddie,' said Pippa, rattling the pushchair towards playgroup. 'I'm going to ring for help. Can you walk a few steps ahead of me, please?'

The call connected almost immediately. 'Hello, emergency services, which service do you require?'

‘Ambulance, please.’

‘Hold on.’ The phone clicked through and Pippa listened to her heart thudding.

‘Ambulance service, what’s the address of the emergency?’

‘Um, it’s on the meadow behind the shops, in Much Gadding.’

‘On the meadow. What number are you calling from?’

Pippa gave her mobile number.

‘And what has happened?’

‘Someone’s died, we think. Someone has found a body on the meadow and he thinks he’s dead.’

‘Are you with the person?’

‘No, the man who found him is heading back there now.’

‘Oh. How old is the person?’

‘If it’s who he thinks it is, maybe thirty-five.’

‘And they are unconscious?’

‘Um, I’d have thought so. Look, I haven’t seen the person, I’m just ringing this in.’

‘Are you near the area?’

‘I am, but I have my children with me.’ Pippa took a deep breath. ‘Shall I see if I can get someone to watch them, and call you back?’

‘Someone’s already on the way.’ The operator paused. ‘But yes, call back if you can.’

‘I shall. Thanks.’ Pippa ended the call and followed Freddie to the church hall.

‘Thought you’d got lost,’ Imogen joked, then her eyes opened very wide.

‘Can you watch these two for me and get them a snack?’ Pippa said. ‘I’ll be back as soon as I can.’ Without waiting for an answer, she ran to the police station and flung the door open. PC Horsley, behind the desk, was halfway through raising his eyebrows when he saw her expression.

‘Jim, come quickly,’ she said. ‘There’s a body on the meadow.’

PC Horsley sprang up, reached for his keys, and lifted the flap on the counter.

***

Pippa had to run to keep up with the policeman. ‘Has anyone called an ambulance?’ he asked, out of the side of his mouth.

‘I did,’ Pippa panted. ‘They said they’re on the way.’

‘Good.’ He said no more until they had turned down the footpath to the meadow. Malcolm was hovering uncertainly a few feet from a long, low shape just visible in the grass. Otherwise, the meadow was deserted. If Pippa hadn’t known that something was there, she would have missed it. As she approached she could make out blue jeans and a green T-shirt, and finally, the form of a man with longish brown hair, sprawled face-down. He looked as if he had tripped, but his hair was matted with blood.

‘Hello, Malcolm,’ said PC Horsley, squatting beside the body. He touched the man’s wrist, grimaced, then felt for a pulse. ‘This doesn’t look good.’

‘No, it doesn’t,’ said Malcolm, his eyes averted.

‘When did you find him?’

‘A few minutes ago. Say ten to eleven.’

‘Ten to eleven. You’re pretty sure of that?’

Malcolm took a step back. ‘I just went for a stroll, I wasn’t expecting this —’

PC Horsley looked up at him. ‘Of course not, Malcolm. I’m just trying to establish a few facts.’

‘That sounds about right,’ said Pippa. ‘I went to the primary school for a tour, and I left at quarter to. I was coming to playgroup when Malcolm ran across the road.’

Malcolm shot her a grateful look. ‘I was coming to the police station, you see.’

‘I see.’ PC Horsley laid the man’s wrist on the ground, then stood up and took out his notebook. ‘How close did you come to the body?’

‘Not as close as you are now,’ said Malcolm. ‘I touched his hand, felt how cold it was, and ran to fetch someone.’ He shivered and turned away. ‘The blood —’

A brief wail pierced the air, and ceased as abruptly. ‘The ambulance,’ said Pippa.

‘Yes,’ said the policeman. ‘Not that they can do anything for him.’

A paramedic ran onto the meadow and PC Horsley waved her over. As he had done, she bent and checked for a pulse. Then she lifted the wrist, and finally, with both hands, she raised the head a fraction. She shook her head. ‘Rigor mortis has begun; he’s already stiffening. He’s well beyond our reach, I’m afraid.’ She glanced at Pippa. ‘Were you the person who phoned?’

‘That’s right,’ said Pippa. ‘I hadn’t seen him at that point, I was focused on getting help.’

‘Don’t worry,’ said the paramedic. ‘Better that way

round. You did the right thing.' She stood up and turned to the policeman. 'I don't suppose you need us, then.'

'I'm afraid not,' said PC Horsley. 'I'll radio Gadcester station for backup. They'll get a doc over.'

Pippa stared. 'Won't you take him?' she asked the paramedic.

'No, love,' the paramedic replied. 'He's one for the Coroner now, and the police will take care of it. Preserve the crime scene, and all that. Right, I'll be off.' She strode back the way she had come, looking straight ahead.

Malcolm shuddered, and PC Horsley turned to him. 'If you give me a phone number I can reach you at, Malcolm, you can go. I don't think keeping you here is helping anyone. I'll make a note of what you've told me, and we'll be in touch for a more formal statement soon.'

Malcolm's shoulders relaxed. 'Thank you. I doubt I'd make any sense at the moment.' PC Horsley found a fresh page in his notebook, and Malcolm dictated his number, peering as the policeman wrote. 'That's it.'

'Thank you. And I have a phone number for you, too. Both of you, in fact.' PC Horsley wrote on two successive sheets of his notebook, then ripped them out and handed them over. 'This is the Victim Support helpline, and they look after witnesses too.' Malcolm fumbled the paper into his pocket. 'Keep this to yourselves for now, or at least to close family. The last thing we need is a crowd at the gate while we're going about our business.'

Malcolm gaped. 'I don't think I *can* talk about it.'

They watched Malcolm wander away. He took a different path from the paramedic, heading towards the exit by the ford.

'I hope he's OK,' said Pippa. 'He might be in shock.'

'Are you surprised?' said PC Horsley, his eyebrows raised. He pulled out his radio. 'If you don't mind,' he said, rather pointedly.

Pippa walked perhaps twenty feet away, and looked towards the exit which the paramedic had taken. *Should I stay? Am I supposed to go?*

The radio feedback stopped. 'It's called in,' said PC Horsley. 'They're coming.'

'What happens now?'

PC Horsley pursed up his mouth. 'Investigation.' He took his phone from his pocket. 'Photos. They'll bring a camera, but this will have to do for now.' He took several shots of the scene; the dead man, the grass around him, close-ups of the back of his head and his hands. 'Sealing off the area. Post-mortem.' He pocketed the phone and his eyes met hers. 'You can go too, Pippa.'

Pippa's glance flicked down. She was almost sure that the dead man was Tony Green; the build was right, and the watch on his left wrist seemed familiar, but she couldn't be sure. Her curiosity fought with her sense of decency, and the fact that she had dumped her kids at playgroup without explanation. 'Will you tell me if it is Tony Green?'

PC Horsley's face was expressionless. 'This is a police matter, Mrs Parker.'

Pippa felt thoroughly rebuked. 'Of course. I'm sorry.'

As she hurried back to the safety of the pavement and the village Pippa thought of Tony Green, smiling and confident, outlining his vision for the meadow. His face swam into her mind, and now she could see who he resembled — who he had resembled. With his long brown hair, beard and pale blue eyes, he had looked like Aragorn from the *Lord of the Rings* films. And now — she didn't want to think about it. At the gate, she looked back. Jim Horsley was a small figure, his face turned towards her. Hopefully he wouldn't have to wait long for help.

Pippa checked her watch as she emerged onto the road. A quarter past eleven. It felt as if much, much more time had passed. Her wrist trembled as she held it up, and she let it fall by her side. She crossed the road, looking both ways, and headed to playgroup. On one hand she desperately wanted to be back in normal surroundings, thinking of nothing more pressing than whether Ruby needed changing, or whether there would still be hot water in the urn. On the other — she swallowed, and her throat hurt — how was she going to appear normal for the next three-quarters of an hour?

She took a deep breath, grasped the door handle, and went in.

***

As it turned out, she needn't have worried. Her arrival barely registered with the group. The toddlers and preschoolers carried on playing as normal, while their parents and carers sat in a semicircle, at the centre of which were Sam and Imogen.

'And she said what about extending the school?' Caitlin asked.

'Well,' Sam leaned forward confidentially. 'She said she couldn't see it happening, as Much Gadding wouldn't have enough families to fill a school double the size.'

General scoffing from the group. 'It practically could now!' said Eva.

Pippa looked for her children. Freddie and Henry were playing with Livvy; but instead of being glued to the garage as they usually were, Henry was making shaky letters on a blackboard with chalk, while Livvy shouted 'That's it! Good boy, Henry!' Ruby, meanwhile, was sitting on the rug with Freddie, who had an arm round her back to steady her. Pippa considered going in for a cuddle, but they were so wrapped up in their game that she didn't want to disturb them.

Imogen waved. 'They've been fine,' she said. 'They've both had a drink and a biscuit. Hope that's OK.' And she turned back to the debate.

'I'll go and see if there's any hot water,' said Pippa, to no-one, and went to the kitchen. Monika, a new recruit to the playgroup, was washing up. 'Want a hand?' Pippa asked. The hatch was open, so she could watch the children, be useful, and stay away from the conversation all at the same time.

'Yes please,' said Monika. 'A cloth is over there if you would like to dry.' Monika was tall and blonde, and her English was formal. In some ways Pippa was guiltily glad that Monika, nice as she seemed, was in Much Gadding only while her husband completed a year's secondment in a Gadcester engineering firm.

'Is there any hot water in the urn?' she asked.

Monika clicked her tongue slightly. 'You have missed the tea break.'

Pippa fetched the tea towel and began to dry the cups and saucers on the draining board.

'The headteacher said there wasn't money to extend the school,' Imogen commented.

'She's probably right about that,' said Caitlin. 'The council never have money for anything useful, like filling in potholes or sorting out the buses.'

The group rumbled. Pippa put one dry cup inside another.

'And if the houses on the meadow *do* go ahead —'

The saucer Pippa was drying slipped through her fingers and fell on the worktop with a clatter. Monika sucked her breath in, and everyone stared at the hatch. 'Sorry,' muttered Pippa. 'Carry on.' She inspected the saucer, which was undamaged, put it down, and reached for another. But tears swam in her eyes, and she couldn't wipe them away, not in full view of the room. 'Excuse me,' she said, stepping back, 'I need the bathroom.'

Pippa forced herself to walk, not run out of the kitchen, and to hold herself together until she was safely locked in a cubicle. Then she let the tears flow.

*It's probably shock,* she told herself.

If only Lila didn't work on a Thursday. She could have come on the school tour, or at least been there to confide in. She would have seen that something was wrong, and found tea —

Maybe she could text Simon, if she told him not to tell anyone. Pippa reached into her bag for her phone, but what she saw on the screen stopped her in her tracks.

On a previous case PC Horsley had given her his

mobile number, in case she had anything to report privately. Since he'd asked her to keep it secret, she had codenamed him Piglet in her address book.

And now her home screen bore the legend *Piglet: DELETE THIS — it was.*

Piglet had squealed.

# CHAPTER 8

In the end it was Simon who texted her, at lunchtime. *How was school? x*

Pippa briefly wondered where to begin, then settled for *Was OK let's chat when kids in bed x*

*Not that good then?*

*Still thinking it over,* she replied. Frankly, given what had happened afterwards, it had paled into insignificance. *That poor, poor man,* she had thought while dishing up lunch, giving extra care to the arrangement of chicken fingers, chips and beans on the children's plates. *I don't even know if he had a wife and family.*

And if he didn't, there was no chance of that now. Tony Green, back in Much Gadding, planning to build an ambitious new development which could have done the village some good —

Perhaps she was romanticising, given what she knew now. But he had seemed so young and idealistic, and all those dreams had come to nothing.

Pippa shook her head, and took the plates into the dining room, where Freddie stirred everything together and Ruby, with great concentration, picked up a piece of chicken finger and threw it on the floor.

After lunch she loaded the children into the Mini and drove to the park in Gadding Magna, where Freddie swung as high as he dared (not very) and Ruby giggled while she sat in the baby swing. That, and an ice cream, took care of an hour and a half, by which time Ruby was grizzling for a nap and Freddie was muttering that *SuperMouse* would be on soon.

They headed home, and once everyone was settled Pippa made a cup of tea (with a Jammie Dodger on the side as shock treatment), went into the dining room, and unlocked her phone.

*Tony Green Construction*, she typed into the search engine.

Surprisingly for such a common name, he was at the top of the results. Not because of what she and a very few other people knew; but because of his popular website. There was a photo of him accepting an award, wearing a wide grin and more or less the same outfit as he had worn at the village meeting, and one of him with his arm round a slim blonde woman who reminded Pippa faintly of Monika, except her smile was broader.

Pippa navigated to the website and clicked on *About Tony Green.*

*I grew up in the lovely village of Much Gadding in leafy Gadcestershire, before moving to York with my family when I was sixteen.*

*Back then I didn't know what I wanted to do, apart from save the world.*

Pippa could feel tears coming. She rubbed the corners of her eyes with her forefingers, and scrolled down.

*When I dropped out of college I ended up working on a building site — and that was what showed me the way. I did a course or two, looked for like-minded people, and soon I had assembled a posse of eco-builders. We began with small jobs like extensions, and grew from there.*

*It was when I was consulting with a local school about harnessing green energy that I met my lovely fiancée, Leanne. We're planning to set a wedding date soon, but between school terms and my growing business, we're finding it hard!*

Pippa closed her browser, locked her phone, and put it face-down on the table. She couldn't read any more. She didn't want to think about it any more. She fetched her laptop from its place on the sideboard, opened it, and pulled up the events spreadsheet she had created for Lady Higginbotham's concert series. She needed something to lose herself in.

***

By the time Simon got home the children had been fed again and put to bed, and Pippa was two-thirds of the way through a large to-do list. 'Sorry I'm late,' he said, walking into the dining room and kissing her. 'I was finishing up the Zen Diagrams paperwork and then Gerald wanted a word. And then I got stuck in traffic outside the village.'

Pippa looked up at him. 'Whereabouts?'

'Roughly a mile from the Hall. Turned out there was a

big queue at the roundabout by Polly's. I don't think they've closed the road to Parva, but something was slowing people down.'

Pippa grimaced. 'If I tell you, will you promise not to tell anyone?'

Simon frowned. 'Tell anyone what?' He sat opposite.

Pippa closed the laptop. 'Seriously, do you promise, at least for now?'

He sighed. 'Of course I promise.'

She met his eyes. 'Tony Green was murdered on the meadow this morning.'

'*What?*' Simon's jaw dropped. 'Are you sure?'

Pippa nodded. 'I saw him. Face down, but I was almost sure it was him. And PC Horsley confirmed it.'

'Oh my God.' Simon got up and paced, and Pippa thought how odd it was that people really did do things that you saw in films. He paused, and looked at her. 'Are you OK?'

'I — think so.' Pippa wasn't sure, but given that she wasn't curled up in a ball weeping, she figured she was probably over the worst.

Simon sat beside Pippa and put an arm round her shoulders, and a wail grew inside her like a wave. She buried her head in his chest to steady herself. 'I *was* OK, till you did that!' she gasped. 'Aaaha-ha-ha-haaaa…'

He held her, rocking her gently, until she had wept most of it out, then stroked her damp hair back from her face. 'You could have phoned me, you know. Or asked me to come home. I would have.'

'I know, but you were busy, and I had the kids, and —

it was just easier to cope.'

He was silent, studying her face. 'How come you were on the meadow?' he asked. 'You — the kids weren't with you, were they?'

'Oh God, no,' she said. 'I was heading for playgroup after the school visit when Malcolm Allason came running from the meadow as if the Hound of the Baskervilles was chasing him. He nearly got run over. I stopped him and he told me what he'd found, so I told him to go and stay with the — body. I rang an ambulance, dropped the kids at playgroup, then fetched Jim Horsley.'

Simon's mouth twitched. 'Well, I suppose if anyone knows what to do in the event of a murder, it's you.'

'*Simon!*'

'Sorry.' He pinched the bridge of his nose. 'I'm just — I can't take it in. I mean, Tony Green. He can't be more than, what, thirty-five, thirty-six?'

'I know.' A sigh shuddered out of her. 'That's why you got stuck in traffic. The meadow will be a crime scene. People rubbernecking even though there's nothing to see.'

'And it's definitely murder?'

'It couldn't be anything else. I saw blood on the back of his head. But you can't tell anyone. Definitely not until it's common knowledge, anyway.'

'That won't take long round here,' Simon remarked.

'And that goes double for Sheila,' said Pippa. 'She'll be fuming that I was on the scene when she does find out. She hasn't forgiven me for fitting in another case while she was in Tenerife, you know.'

'You might have mentioned it,' said Simon. 'Joking

aside, what do you want to do about dinner? You look as if you've been busy.'

'Distracting myself, mostly.' Pippa tapped the laptop. 'It's amazing how much work you can do when you're avoiding something else.'

'I'll see what we've got in.' Pippa got up and followed Simon to the kitchen, where he crouched in front of the freezer. 'Lasagne?'

Pippa pictured meat and tomato sauce, and shuddered. 'Is it veg lasagne?'

Simon pulled out the packet and inspected it. 'Nope.'

'Maybe not. There's a chicken korma for two on the second shelf.'

Simon reached in and retrieved a package, pushing aside the frosting to read the name. 'There is. That do?'

'That'll do.'

He closed the freezer door, put the box on the worktop, and took Pippa's hands. The chill on his made her flinch. 'If you need to go and talk to someone —'

'I'll get over it. It was just — so unexpected. I didn't even see the worst. Poor Malcolm looked haunted.'

'I bet he did.'

'When he first said he'd found something…' Pippa snorted, 'I thought he meant a fossil.' Her shoulders shook.

'Oh dear…' Simon put his arms round Pippa as she half-giggled, half-cried. 'You should get a doctor's appointment. Or find a counselling service. Maybe see if Jim Horsley can recommend someone.'

Pippa pulled back. 'What, with the kids?'

'I know.' HIs voice was soft, soothing, just a little

annoying. 'See how you feel in a couple of days.'

'OK. PC Horsley gave me a phone number to ring. I'll try that, maybe.' She gave him a squeeze, then gently disengaged herself. 'Come on, let's get this in the microwave. I'm knackered. Too much slaving over a hot laptop.'

Simon slid the cardboard sleeve off the box and read the back. 'OK.' He opened the fridge and handed Pippa a bottle of beer. 'Why don't you take care of that, and I'll manage the food.'

Pippa raised an eyebrow, opened the beer, and wandered into the lounge. As she did so she heard the unmistakable sound of a fork piercing plastic film. *Bless him*, she thought. *He probably thinks I'll have a meltdown if I witness him stabbing a korma.*

She switched the TV on and flicked through the channels. Police drama — no. Someone renovating a barn — no. She watched a cookery programme for a couple of minutes, until the chef started bashing a piece of meat with a mallet. She settled on an antiques show, and was just getting into it when Simon came in with two plates. 'Eating in here, then?' he said.

'We can go into the dining room, I don't mind.'

'You've probably been in there working long enough.' He sat next to her and put her plate on the coffee table. 'So . . . school trip?'

The conversation which Pippa had thought would be difficult was easy now. 'The school seemed nice. I didn't warm to the headteacher though. And she said they're not planning to extend it.'

Simon chased a piece of chicken with his fork. 'It probably doesn't matter as much now.' He paused. 'But you liked the school.'

'Yes. The pupils looked happy, and the deputy head was — a bit more approachable.' She had been going to say *nice*, but Emma Knight was friendly, knowledgeable, helpful. Nice didn't convey any of that. It was more the sort of word that Sheila would use of a woman like Shelley Jackson. 'I don't suppose — no, of course not.'

'Of course not what?'

'Mrs Jackson wouldn't have been the head when you were there.'

'No, Pepperpot was our head. Mr Philpott. Short, fat and shouty. Mrs Jackson was there, though. Her class were really noisy.'

'Were they?' That didn't sound much like the woman she had met.

'Mm-hm.' Simon put the captured piece of chicken into his mouth and chewed, musing. 'I can't imagine her as a headteacher.'

'Well, she said she'd been head for fifteen years, so she can't be bad.'

'Is that a vote of confidence I hear?' Simon smiled.

Pippa scooped up some rice and sauce. 'I suppose.'

# CHAPTER 9

The next day the murder was the talk of the village. *BUILDING TYCOON SAVAGELY MURDERED!* screamed the *Messenger*, and the *Gadcester Chronicle* led with *MUCH GADDING MAN BATTERED TO DEATH IN VILLAGE CENTRE.* Of course the articles were shared on social media, and Pippa blinked as notifications flashed at the top of her phone screen. *Caitlin has tagged you in a post... New message from Eva...* She put her phone down and went to make a cup of tea.

Downstairs, she opened her laptop while the kettle boiled and read the stories on the newspapers' websites. Neither of them had much to report, as yet. The bare facts were that a body identified as being that of Tony Green, 36, had been found on the meadow at 10.50am, and that he had been beaten around the head and face by a hard and probably heavy object, which was not found at the scene. A forensic post-mortem was being carried out. In the meantime, anyone who might have information related to the crime was urged to contact Inspector Fanshawe at Gadcester police station.

*Why not Jim Horsley?* thought Pippa. Then again, this was a violent and deliberate crime. She had no idea of how police procedure worked, but maybe something like this moved up to the next level. At least she hadn't been mentioned in either article. If she had — The thought of the questions she might have been asked was enough to make her retch. Instead, she shut the laptop and realised that she hadn't heard the kettle ping.

Simon held her phone up when she came into the bedroom with the tea. 'I put it on silent,' he said. 'I hope you don't mind, it was like a pinball game.'

'Oh God.' She handed him his tea in exchange for the phone and braced herself. Ten notifications and eight new messages. The latest was from Imogen. *When you asked me to look after the kids yesterday…?* followed by a thinking face emoji.

*It was related*, she replied, *but please don't tell anyone. I don't know any more than what's in the papers.*

She sighed and went through her notifications. Most people had tagged her without comment, although Sam had written *Another one for you Pippa!* and someone she knew in passing had replied to Sam: *Deerstalker time?*

Well, if that was the worst she should probably be grateful.

Then her phone rang. *Number unknown.* Pippa's finger hovered over the *Decline* button, but . . . what if it was something important? What if it was Inspector Fanshawe, or someone with information? She pressed *Accept.*

‘Oh hello,’ said a smooth female voice, ‘is that Mrs Pippa Parker?’

‘It is, yes,’ said Pippa, warily.

‘Thank you for answering your phone, I know it’s early but I wasn’t sure what would be the best time to catch you —’

‘Um, who am I speaking to?’

‘This is Janey Dixon from the *Gadcester Chronicle*. I wondered if you would like to comment on the terrible murder which has happened in Much Gadding.’

‘The murder?’ Pippa said, playing for time. *Why is Janey Dixon ringing me?* She had had a sinking feeling the moment the name was said. She and Janey Dixon, opinion columnist for the *Chronicle*, had history, and while she had managed to write a comparatively nice piece about Lady Higginbotham’s afternoon teas, Pippa didn’t trust her past the end of her pointy nose.

‘Yes, the murder,’ Janey Dixon said, a little crossly.

‘What makes you think I have anything to say about a murder?’ Pippa sipped her tea, loud enough for it to be audible to her caller.

‘You do have a little habit that way,’ said Janey, and Pippa heard a smug little smile in her voice. ‘And when I spoke to Malcolm Allason yesterday, he said that you called an ambulance and fetched the local PC Plod to the scene.’ The smile was now a grin. ‘So yes, I imagine you have opinions.’

‘*If* I do,’ said Pippa, ‘I’ll be keeping them to myself. This is a live investigation, and beyond offering minor assistance I was in no way involved.’

'Mmm,' said Janey. 'We'll be printing Malcolm's interview tomorrow, once we've run it past Gadcester Police. I'm fairly sure he mentions you by name. *Good*bye, Mrs Parker.' And she hung up.

Pippa shouted a rude word and was aiming her phone at the wall when Simon took it out of her hand. 'What's up, Pip?' he asked, putting the phone on his bedside table, out of her reach.

'Bloody Janey Dixon, that's what. She was digging for titbits, and because I wouldn't give her any, she's going to make sure my name gets in tomorrow's paper. Oooooh, I could —'

'You won't, though.'

She sighed. 'No.'

'What are your plans for the day?' Simon asked. 'I need to get going. Big lunch meeting in Brum, and a pre-meeting meeting for us beforehand.' He took a shirt from the wardrobe and scrutinised it. 'Not sure if it's a tie or no-tie day.'

'On a Friday? Surely you can get away with no tie.'

'Not sure. I'll take one with me.' He opened the drawer where he kept them and gazed at the neat rolls, like a collection of sleeping snakes. 'Anyway. You?'

'Freddie to preschool, of course —'

'Of course. And then?'

'A bit more work, if Rubes will let me. I've practically got the Proms at the Hall organised, so if I can get Lady H to sign it off, we're cooking with gas.'

'And…?'

Pippa looked up at his expectant face. 'What do you

mean, and?'

'School…?'

'Yes. Try to book a couple more school visits.' She sipped her tea. 'It is on my radar, but with everything else —'

'I know. I just don't want us — well, Freddie — to miss the boat.'

Pippa's vision of Freddie punting down the River Gad in a straw boater floated into her mind, and it was all she could do not to snigger. 'Absolutely not,' she said, hastily. 'But I'm planning to lay low. The last thing I want is to be mobbed by a bunch of locals asking me who I think dunnit.'

'Wise move.' Simon knotted his tie and checked it in the mirror, then shrugged on his suit jacket. 'I'll get off, otherwise I'll end up parked a mile from the station.' He leaned down and kissed the top of her head. 'If you need to talk, call me. It might go to voicemail, but I *will* call you back.'

'Thanks,' said Pippa, hoping that she wouldn't need to talk.

***

Pippa dropped Freddie off at preschool ten minutes early. Mrs Marks sucked her cheeks in a little when she came to the door, but accepted Freddie without overt comment. 'Off somewhere, are we?' she asked, eyeing the large clock on the wall which was the sole arbiter of preschool time.

'No, no, just a quiet morning at home,' said Pippa. 'My watch must be fast.' She hurried along the path with Ruby in her arms, and got into the car herself as another car slowed down and indicated. She looked straight ahead and started the engine. Whoever it was would have to manage without a *good morning* today.

Conversely, Pippa had a very good morning. She took the laptop into the lounge and wrote emails while Ruby tortured her activity centre and made various attempts to crawl into trouble, then put Ruby down for a nap and made follow-up calls.

'There,' she said, nodding at her phone. 'Now for Lady H.'

She pulled together an email with dates, performers, estimated costings, and what had been provisionally booked, and sent it to Lady Higginbotham's email address (it never failed to amaze her that Lady Higginbotham actually had one). Then she rang the hall, since while Lady Higginbotham had an email address, she never checked it without being prompted.

'Higginbotham Hall, Mrs Harbottle speaking,' said Beryl, in her best phone voice.

'Hello Beryl, it's Pippa Parker. I've just sent an email through confirming dates, acts, and prices for the Proms.'

'Ooo!' said Beryl. 'I'll put you through.' A series of push-button tones followed, then Beryl's normal voice saying 'It's Pippa on the line, she's sorted the concerts out,' followed by a *beep-beep*.

'Good morning, Pippa,' said June Higginbotham, sounding very pleased.

'Good morning, Lady Higginbotham.'

'Beryl says you've sent me an *email*.' She pronounced

the word as if it was the oddest thing Pippa could possibly have done. 'Would you like to pop over, and we can talk it through?'

'So long as I leave in time to fetch Freddie, yes that's fine.'

'Lovely. We'll see you in a few minutes then.'

Upstairs, Ruby was beginning to stir. 'Come on, trouble,' Pippa said to the long eyelashes fluttering on the pink cheeks. 'We're off to the big house.' She suspected the prompt invitation meant Lady Higginbotham had forgotten her email password again, but a visit to the hall would be a nice safe trip out for them both before collecting Freddie. And if it meant more business, so much the better.

***

'So nice to see you,' said Lady Higginbotham, opening the door to Pippa herself. She did seem unusually smug, like a cat who had not only got the cream, but finished it. 'We'll use the morning room.'

Pippa had never visited this part of the house; previously she had been confined to the dining room or the hall. She gazed around her at the paintings, the beautiful oak panelling, and the damp spreading outwards from the window.

'It's next on the list,' said Lady Higginbotham. But she seemed cheerful even in the face of house repairs.

Pippa parked Ruby in a safe spot for her host's china, then sat at the table, opened her laptop, and showed Lady Higginbotham the email she had sent, pointing to the dates, the amounts, and the profit estimate. Usually Lady

Higginbotham erred very much on the side of caution; but today she waved a hand at the screen. 'It looks wonderful to me,' she said airily. 'Go for it, Pippa.'

'Lady Higginbotham,' said Pippa, 'can I ask you something?'

'Of course!' said Lady Higginbotham. 'And you know you're supposed to call me June.' Her tone was indulgent.

'June…' Pippa considered, then decided to go for it. 'You seem happy today.'

'Oh, I *am*,' said Lady Higginbotham. 'A weight's been taken off my mind. Although not in the most pleasant of circumstances.' She rose, walked to the sideboard, and picked up a copy of the *Gadcester Chronicle*. It was that morning's — Pippa could tell by the headline, which Lady Higginbotham tapped with a pale oval fingernail.

'You mean Tony Green?' Pippa felt as if her eyes would pop out of her head.

'I'm afraid I do,' said Lady Higginbotham. 'It isn't that I wished the man any harm, but he was so — so plausible at the consultation meeting. I was convinced that his plan to build on the meadow would go ahead. And now I assume that will all go away.'

'But why would you mind about the meadow?'

Lady Higginbotham's cheeks had flushed a delicate rose. 'It probably sounds selfish, but look.' She walked over to the window, and Pippa followed. 'Do you see, in the distance?'

Pippa screwed her eyes up to see where she was pointing. Past the lawn, and the track to the main road, between the war memorial and the silver ribbon of the

River Gad — there was the long grass of the meadow.

'It's always been there,' said Lady Higginbotham. 'It isn't very exciting, but it's been part of my landscape — well, all my life.' She breathed out a long, slow breath. 'And there's another reason. Do you see those outbuildings?' She indicated a pair of tumbledown shacks. 'I'm thinking of renovating those as holiday cottages. Let's face it, would you rent a place with a view of some weird eco-hub?' She looked at Pippa. 'Of course not,' she said. 'People want unspoilt countryside, not a building site on their doorstep.'

'Mmm,' said Pippa. 'I really had better go and get Freddie.'

'What I just said is between you, me and Beryl, you understand.' An anxious shadow crossed Lady Higginbotham's face. 'As I said, I certainly didn't wish the poor man any ill.'

'Of course not,' said Pippa, wondering if her tone sounded as flat to Lady Higginbotham as it did to her. 'But you're happy for me to get on with booking for the concerts? And promoting them?'

'Oh yes,' said Lady Higginbotham, with a look of relief on her face. 'Please do.'

'Great,' said Pippa. 'I'll be in touch.'

When she got back to the Mini, she found that in the twenty minutes or so she had been away a bird had done its business on the roof. It summed up Pippa's mood. *Just as I thought I was getting a handle on things, someone craps all over it.*

Even after she had loaded Ruby in and stowed her

belongings, she still had time to spare before collecting Freddie. Pippa turned the radio up loud and drove aimlessly for ten minutes along the winding country roads. *It shouldn't matter what Lady H thinks*, she told herself. *She's your client, not your friend.*

But she did count June Higginbotham as a sort of friend. As someone she was well-disposed towards, whom she would have a cup of tea and chat with if the opportunity presented itself. She trusted June Higginbotham to be the sort of person who would *do the right thing*.

And now, she wasn't so sure.

# CHAPTER 10

Pippa's phone shrilled from her bag as she was making bananas and custard for the children. *Unknown number.* Mindful of her earlier encounter with Janey Dixon, she moved away from the stove and made sure no sharp objects were nearby before answering.

'Is that Mrs — Pippa Parker?' asked a nervous man's voice.

'It might be,' said Pippa. 'It depends who's calling. If you're flogging solar panels then no, I'm not.'

Silence at the other end of the line. 'This is Constable Gannet from Gadcester Police Station.'

*Darn.* 'Sorry about that,' said Pippa. 'What can I do for you?'

'We'd like you to come in and answer some questions concerning your movements on the morning of the twenty-eighth of September, Mrs Parker.' PC Gannet sounded much surer of himself now that he was back to the script.

'OK. When?'

'Any time this afternoon.'

'I'm afraid not, PC Gannet, I'm at home with my children.'

'Oh.' Another pause. 'Can't someone babysit them for you?'

'Can't it wait until I've had time to arrange childcare?' Pippa countered.

'You don't seem to think this is an important matter, Mrs Parker,' said PC Gannet. 'I assure you that it is, though. Very important.' Pippa could picture him leaning back in his chair, smiling to himself.

'I'm happy to come in and give a statement,' said Pippa. 'I just don't think my almost-four year old is quite ready to be privy to the details of a murder.' She paused. 'I can come in on Monday at eleven o'clock if that's any good.'

'Let me check the calendar,' said PC Gannet, his feet now firmly off the desk in Pippa's imagination. 'Yes. Eleven sharp, Mrs Parker. Let us know if you need anything.'

'See you then, constable,' said Pippa, and rang off. It was only afterwards, while the children were stuffing dripping yellow spoonfuls into their faces, that she realised —

The call had come from PC Gannet, not Jim Horsley.

She'd been asked to go to Gadcester station, not Much Gadding.

And she hadn't been asked to make a statement.

She'd been asked to *answer some questions.*

Pippa's initial reaction was to hold her hands up in a

*not me, guv* style. Her next was to dismiss it as PC Gannet's self-important tosh.

But all the same, she made a mental note to be on time next Monday.

***

Once lunch was over, and the children in a hazy slump of carbohydrate overload, Pippa went back to work in the lounge, balancing her laptop on her knees. After all, the Proms at the Hall wouldn't promote themselves. She wrote a brief press release and emailed it to the *Chronicle,* the *Messenger*, and the local radio stations, who mostly worked out of the same building in the centre of Gadcester. With any luck, the concerts might get into the What's On section.

What she didn't expect was yet another phone call half an hour later. The contact said *Media Desk Gadcester Chron etc.*

'Good afternoon, Pippa Parker speaking,' she said, aiming for brisk professionalism. Especially after the PC Gannet conversation.

'Oh hello Pippa,' said a bright voice. 'It's Julie from the PR team at Gadcester FM. I've just been reading your press release about the concerts at Higginbotham Hall. Would you be able to phone into Ritz Robertson's show tomorrow morning to talk about them? Maybe at eight am-ish?'

'That would be wonderful!' exclaimed Pippa. 'Of course I shall.' Then something struck her. 'Would you rather have Lady Higginbotham herself? I could ask —'

'Lady Higginbotham is rather publicity-shy,' said Julie.

'To be honest, I think you'll do a better job of promoting the concerts. I mean, you know all the detail.'

'I suppose I do.' The smile left Pippa's face as she realised how smug she sounded, and how like Lady Higginbotham this morning.

'I'll give you a direct number to call. Oh, and if you could have some further information to hand — about the bands, maybe.'

'Absolutely,' said Pippa. 'Thank you so much, Julie.'

'No, thank *you*, Pippa,' Julie replied.

Once the call was ended, Pippa punched the air. *Yes!* Ritz Robertson's breakfast show was the most popular in Gadcestershire. Maybe she could even talk him into acting as MC for a concert or two. And if he said he would do it on air, then he'd have to. She caught herself doing a victory dance, and stopped abruptly.

***

Pippa was already awake when her alarm went off at a quarter to seven the next morning. She had gone to bed early the night before, and refused Simon's offer of celebratory wine on the grounds that she needed to be sharp. *There*, she thought triumphantly, switching off the 7.00, 7.15, and 7.30 alarms she had set as a precaution. She bounced out of bed and startled Simon awake. 'Ersmerrrwha time is it?' One eye opened slightly.

'Don't worry, you don't have to be up yet,' said Pippa. 'I'm going to make a coffee.'

'Saright then,' he murmured, embedding himself more deeply in the pillow. 'Crackodawn.'

Pippa tiptoed downstairs. She hadn't told Freddie what

was happening that morning, and she wanted to keep it under wraps until her segment was done. While Simon had been briefed, and no doubt would do his best to contain the children, she had a feeling that if Freddie found out she was on the radio he would find a way to make himself heard. She closed the kitchen door and filled the kettle fuller than it needed to be so that it would boil less noisily, apologising to the environment as she did so for the waste of resources. Tony Green popped into her head, and she tried to dismiss him by getting the milk from the fridge.

Pippa kept Tony Green at bay by going through the notes she had made the day before. She had her email *and* her spreadsheet open on the laptop (which she had charged, just in case). She had also written notes as backup, which contained the key points she wanted to get across, the best-known songs of each act, and the biggest venue they had performed in to date.

'How long will you be on air?' Simon had asked, as she ripped another sheet from her pad and numbered it.

Pippa shrugged. 'Five minutes, maybe ten?'

'You don't think you're over-preparing a tiny bit?' he had asked.

'There's no such thing when you're doing a live broadcast,' Pippa said, trying to sound as if being on the radio was second nature.

'Well, it's your show, Pippa,' Simon had said, retreating to the lounge. 'For five minutes, anyway.'

Everything remained blissfully quiet until Pippa's 7.45 alarm shrilled on her phone. Admittedly, she had turned the volume up a tiny bit to make sure she didn't miss it.

But while it still wasn't particularly loud, the effect was electric. 'What was that?' shouted Freddie.

'Calm down, Freddie, it's just Mummy's alarm ringing.'

'But why? It's Saturday! We don't have alarms on Saturday.'

'Not usually, no. Mummy has something to do.'

'What?' Quick feet ran to the head of the stairs. 'Mummy? What are you doing?'

Next, a wail from Ruby's room, which was the thing Pippa had dreaded most. Freddie, potentially, could be reasoned with and bribed to keep quiet if need be. A baby was a different matter entirely. 'Thanks, Freddie,' she muttered to herself. Then, thinking more practically, she filled two sippy cups with water, grabbed a packet of rusks, and ran upstairs.

'Simon, administer these,' she said.

Simon raised an eyebrow. 'What's the magic word, Pip?'

'Please. *Pleease.* Pretty please with a cherry on top.'

'That'll do.' He grinned and Pippa stuck her tongue out at him before bolting downstairs. Her phone display said 7.49. Plenty of time to calm them down.

Except Ruby wasn't calming down. 'She doesn't like really cold water, Pippa, you know that,' Simon called wearily.

'Fine,' snapped Pippa. 7.52 now, and Ruby was screaming at the top of her lungs. She gave it one more minute, and as Ruby was still in full flow, charged upstairs again. 'I can't ring the show with this going on.'

'What do you want me to do, put a sock in her mouth?'

Simon was cuddling Ruby and stroking her head, but even that wasn't working.

'I don't know.' Pippa ran a hand through her hair and wished she'd taken a shower. 'Maybe get their coats on and take them into the garden?'

Simon looked incredulous, then resigned. 'OK,' he muttered. 'Don't stay on the phone too long, you might find us frozen outside.' Then he brightened. 'Or we could stay inside and you could take your phone into the garden.'

'Um, the laptop? My notes?' Pippa demanded. She checked the time on her phone (7.54) and saw the low charge light. 'Oh my God, my battery's nearly dead!'

'That'll be a no, then,' Simon muttered as she ran downstairs.

***

Pippa shifted from foot to foot as Simon buttoned coats, buttered toast, and told the children they were going to have an adventure. 'Do you need the loo, Pippa?' he asked, pointedly.

Pippa gave him a *you're not helping* look.

'The world won't end if you ring at 8.02, you know,' he said, opening the back door. 'Come on kids, breakfast in the garden.' He stepped outside, carrying the now-quiet Ruby, and closed the door behind him.

Pippa locked it to make sure before picking up her phone, now tethered to a plug socket in the dining room, and scrolling down the contacts list to the number Julie had given her. While it rang she tried to breathe deeply, stuck a smile on her face, and spread her notes out on the floor. It wasn't exactly what she had envisaged, but it would have to do.

'Hello Gadcester FM, Jake speaking.'

'Hi Jake, this is Pippa Parker. I was asked to phone at eight —'

'Oh yes.' The voice sounded young and Londonish. 'Ritz has just put a song on. I'll tell him you're on the line and take you off hold when it's finishing. Try not to make any noise until Ritz has introduced you.'

'OK,' said Pippa, happily. Hold music played, and she scanned through her main points yet again —

'And that was Taylor Swift,' intoned the cheery tones of Ritz Robertson. 'Now, returning to today's phone-in topic on the rise in rural crime, we have a caller on the line. Pippa Parker, are you there?'

Pippa's mouth fell open.

'Are you there?' Ritz repeated, sounding a little less jolly.

Pippa wished she'd thought of getting a glass of water; her mouth was dry as a bone. 'Yes, I'm here,' she half-croaked.

'I'll turn the mike up a bit,' said Ritz. 'So, Pippa — may I call you Pippa? — the residents of Much Gadding and the surrounding area know you've had a bit of experience with, um, murder. What do you make of what's happened in Much Gadding?'

'I don't make anything of it,' said Pippa. 'I was invited on the show to talk about the concert series we're organising at Higginbotham Hall next month, not to participate in a phone-in.'

'But you must have an opinion,' said Ritz. 'I mean,

Much Gadding is hardly a tourist destination at the moment, with a murderer on the loose.'

'I'm sure the police are doing all they can,' said Pippa, grimly.

'And are you helping them with their enquiries? Today's *Chronicle* says that you summoned the police to the scene.'

Pippa's free hand clenched itself. 'Another person found the body. I just provided assistance.'

'Mmm. Got any theories on whodunnit?'

'No!' Pippa's voice sounded loud even to herself. 'And if I had, I wouldn't put a police investigation in jeopardy by sharing them on a radio show!'

'All right, only asking,' said Ritz. 'So tell me about these concerts.'

Pippa ran through her main points, rather grumpily.

'That's a good night out and no mistake,' said Ritz. 'I must say that Lady Higginbotham's game, putting on events at a time like this. Thank you for calling, Pippa.'

The line went dead. Ritz Robertson would be putting a song on, or saying 'And now to our next caller,' but it didn't matter. She had been stitched up, live on the radio. She could see Janey Dixon walking through the media office, twitching her press release out of Julie's hand, and smiling.

A message flashed up on her phone. *Just heard you on the radio! Sam x*

And another, from Caitlin: *I can't believe you went on Ritz Robertson's show and didn't tell me!*

And yet another, from Lila: *Are you OK? Text me x*

Pippa stretched up to put her phone on the table. The

tapping on the kitchen door became more insistent. She got to her feet and padded through to find her family looking woebegone on the other side of the glass. When she opened the door they burst in. 'It's *cold*, Mummy!' Freddie said accusingly. 'And I want breakfast. Proper breakfast, not toast.'

Simon had Ruby snuggled in his coat. 'How did it go?' he asked. Then he saw her expression and his face changed in response.

'Yeah, that's about right,' said Pippa.

'Are you OK?' he asked, and she shrugged. She couldn't tell him with the children there, and to be honest, she didn't want to.

# CHAPTER 11

Pippa felt rather odd as she got out of her car outside Gadcester police station. Loose, untethered, like a balloon skimming along the ground ready to float away at any moment.

She had spent the weekend firmly in the bosom of her family, and off social media. She had planned to set up events on Facebook, but given the comments she might receive — perhaps not. Updating the Higginbotham Hall website could wait, too. *So much for the publicity boost from an appearance on the radio*, she thought sourly. June Higginbotham hadn't contacted her, and Pippa wasn't sure if it was because she was annoyed that Pippa hadn't made a better job of it, or because she'd missed it, or — Anyway, she wasn't going to commit any of Lady Higginbotham's money, or her own time, until she was sure the concerts were going ahead. As things were right now, and with Ritz Robertson's helpful observations, she couldn't tell.

And Sheila was annoyed. Pippa had texted her at the

weekend to ask if she could still take Ruby on Monday, and had received a somewhat chilly response. Unless there was another way you could read *Oh hello. Wondered when you'd get in touch. Understand you've been busy. Yes fine.*

She was no cheerier in person, taking Ruby at the door with barely a word for Pippa. 'Back before one, yes?' she had said, phrasing it more as an order than a question, and with a brisk nod, closed the door on her.

Pippa gazed at the large red building, ornamented with Victorian scrolls and flourishes, and swallowed. Going in there was a very different proposition from popping down to the little pebble-dashed cube in her village to see Jim Horsley. She imagined cells in the basement, locked with large clanking iron keys. *Stop it, Pippa*, she told herself. *You're here to help, not get banged up.*

The interior of the station was incongruous; modern office furniture and institutional paint and carpeting in a vast high-ceilinged room with plaster mouldings. 'I'm here to give a statement,' she told the officer at the counter. 'Mrs Pippa Parker.'

The officer frowned at her screen. 'Oh yes. Eleven o'clock.' Then she smiled. 'If you take a seat over there, someone will come and fetch you when they're ready.'

Pippa sat on one of the bolted-down plastic chairs and took a magazine from the table. Two other people were waiting; a middle-aged plump man in paint-stained overalls and a woman about Pippa's age in a leather jacket. *Why are they here?* A police officer came from a door at the back and silently claimed the man. Pippa rubbed her arms. Of course it was normal to feel chilly, in such a big room.

The door opened and PC Gannet came into the hall. 'If you'd like to come with me,' he said, and his voice was the confident at-ease version, not the nervous one. *This is his territory*, thought Pippa, and the thought didn't make her feel any better. She had a distinct feeling that PC Gannet, junior as he was, was someone she didn't want to cross. She got up, and followed him out of the hall, down the corridor, to a room labelled *Interview Room C*.

He entered without knocking. Inspector Fanshawe was already in the room, sitting at one corner of the plain wood table. Another chair was placed beside him. Two plain mugs, two notebooks, two pens. A large tape recorder sat in the middle of the table, and a plastic jug of water was on a side table, with a stack of small glasses. The room was warmer than the reception area, but not much.

'Hello, Mrs Parker,' said the Inspector, not looking particularly severe, but not smiling either. 'Take a seat. Would you like a drink?'

'Just water, please,' said Pippa.

PC Gannet went to the side table and poured Pippa a drink, setting it in front of her. 'Would you like one, Inspector?'

'I'll stick with tea, thanks,' said the inspector, sitting back a little. PC Gannet poured out a glass of water for himself and set it next to his mug. Pippa thought about making a comment, something like *Thirsty work*, but she wasn't sure how he'd take it.

Inspector Fanshawe took a long pull at his mug of tea, set it down with a sigh, and sat forward. 'So, here we are again, Mrs Parker.'

‘Yes,’ said Pippa.

‘Another murder in Much Gadding.’

‘Mmm.’

‘As you’ve given a statement before you’ll be familiar with the process. We’ll be recording the conversation,’ — he glanced towards the tape recorder — ‘and PC Gannet and I shall also be taking notes. I’ll give you the official spiel, and then we’ll begin.’

As he went through the formalities Pippa’s attention drifted to PC Gannet, who was drawing a series of 3D boxes in his notebook. He saw Pippa watching, and turned the page.

‘Are we ready?’

‘Yes,’ said Pippa and PC Gannet, together.

‘Good.’ The inspector started the recorder. ‘This is a recording of an interview with Mrs Pippa Parker on the second of October 2017. The time is eleven-oh-eight.’

Pippa confirmed her name, address and date of birth.

‘Can you tell us, in your own words, what happened on the morning of the twenty-eighth of September?’ asked the inspector.

‘Where would you like me to start?’

‘At the beginning of the day, please.’

‘OK. I got up at six thirty because Ruby wanted milk —’

‘And Ruby is…?’ asked the inspector.

‘You know who Ruby is, Inspector,’ said Pippa. ‘You’ve met her several times.’

‘For the benefit of the tape recorder, please,’ said Inspector Fanshawe.

'Ruby is my baby daughter. I made tea and went back to bed, talked to my husband until he left for work, then got breakfast ready at about eight. Usually we would go to playgroup at ten, but we went on a school visit that day, so we walked to Much Gadding primary school for ten o'clock. The tour lasted till a quarter to eleven. I left the school and we were on the way to playgroup when I saw Malcolm Allason running across the road looking strange, and he told me he'd found a body.'

'So up to that point you hadn't visited the meadow?' asked the inspector.

'No.'

'And did you go with him then?'

'No. I told him to go back and stay with the body while I phoned an ambulance and got the police.'

'Mm.' Inspector Fanshawe scribbled in his notebook and pondered it. 'So what happened next?'

'I rang the ambulance on my way to playgroup. Then I asked a friend there to watch the children, and ran round to the police station to get PC Horsley.'

The inspector mused. 'You could have asked for the police when you rang for the ambulance.'

'I suppose I could,' said Pippa. 'But as the police station was round the corner, it made more sense to go there.'

'So you ran to the police station. Do you remember when you arrived?'

'Sorry, no. As you can imagine, I was a bit preoccupied —'

'If you could stick to the facts, Mrs Parker. Can you

remember what you said to PC Horsley?'

Pippa thought. 'It was something like "Come quickly, there's a body on the meadow."'

'And he came straight away?'

'Yes, we went to the meadow together.'

'Right.' Another scribbled note. 'Why did *you* go to the meadow, Mrs Parker?'

'I, um . . . I thought I might be useful. I'd phoned the ambulance, and it seemed right to be there when they arrived. And Malcolm was upset —'

'I'm not surprised.' The inspector underlined a few words. 'Can I clarify something, Mrs Parker?'

'Of course.' *What was coming next?*

'You aren't a police officer, are you?'

'Of course not.'

'And you have never received any police training.'

'No.' *Where's this leading?*

'Have you ever worked as a paramedic, or in a clinical capacity?'

'No, Inspector.'

'You weren't a friend of the deceased?'

'No.' Suddenly the room seemed very warm.

'And you aren't a close friend of Malcolm Allason?'

'I've seen him at the library. He's sort of an acquaintance.' Pippa rubbed her neck. PC Gannet was scribbling furiously.

'When I spoke to the paramedic who came on the scene she said that you were, I quote, "hovering".' The inspector sat back.

'I don't think that's fair,' said Pippa. 'I was probably in

shock, a little, and not sure what to do.'

'Did you know the body was that of Tony Green?'

The inspector was watching her steadily. 'Not at that point. I thought it was, and Malcolm had said that *he* thought it was, but I didn't know until later.' She thought of Jim Horsley's text, and tried not to let it show on her face.

'Can you tell me what happened at the scene while you were present?'

Pippa gave a brief account, which seemed to satisfy the inspector.

'What did you do when you left the scene?'

'I went straight to playgroup.'

The inspector frowned. 'Did you tell them what had happened?'

'Of course not!' Pippa could feel her face burning. 'I said nothing. I told my husband when he got home from work, but no-one else.'

'Mm-hm.' Inspector Fanshawe looked through his notes. As he read, PC Gannet nudged him and murmured something. 'Good point, Constable.' The Inspector looked over at Pippa. 'You said earlier that you arrived at the primary school to go on a tour at ten o'clock. Did you go anywhere else first?'

'No, we didn't.'

'Can you remember when your husband left for work?'

'A quarter to eight, or ten to, maybe.'

'That's quite a gap. And you just stayed at home.'

'Well, yes. You may not know this, Inspector, but raising small children involves lots of small things that take up a disproportionate amount of time. Nappies, breakfast, feeding, washing, getting them dressed, keeping them entertained. I could go on, but I won't.'

'Understood. Your friend, who watched the children for you. Could you give me her name and number, please.'

'You're checking up on me,' said Pippa, uneasily.

'Confirming details,' said the inspector. 'Did you know Tony Green, Mrs Parker?'

Pippa shook her head, then remembered the recorder. 'No, I didn't. I saw him speak at the consultation event, but we had never met apart from that.'

'You didn't know him from the time he lived in Much Gadding, until his teens?'

'No, I grew up in London.' *Please don't ask about my husband.*

'And what did you think of the plans he presented?' The inspector's voice was almost casual.

'I wasn't there long enough to see them. Freddie — my three and a half year old — needed the toilet, so I took the children home before the plans were unveiled.'

'All right. What do you think of his plan to build houses on the meadow?'

Pippa considered her answer. 'I don't use the meadow so that doesn't bother me. My only concern was access to the local primary school.'

'Ah.' The inspector made a note. 'Your older child is three and a half, I see.'

'If you consider that a motive, you might as well arrest all the parents of preschoolers in Much Gadding and have done with it,' said Pippa, perhaps a little more snappishly than she meant. ‘That was a joke, by the way.’

‘Mm. I didn’t find it amusing, I’m afraid.’ The inspector looked up. ‘Oh, and one more thing. I happened to listen to Gadcester FM on Saturday morning.’

Pippa’s head swam, and her grip tightened on the arms of her chair.

‘Did you listen, PC Gannet?’ the inspector asked.

PC Gannet shook his head.

‘Mm. They were doing a phone-in on rural crime, and Mrs Parker rang up —’

‘That was a set-up!’ cried Pippa. ‘They asked me to ring in about a concert series I’m organising, and when I got on the line Ritz Robertson asked me about the murder! I didn’t even know there was a phone-in — I’m not a regular listener!’

‘You didn’t know,’ said Inspector Fanshawe, as he wrote. ‘Ah yes, you did mention some concerts, I recall.’ He finished his sentence with a flourish, and looked up, stern-faced. ‘In that case, Mrs Parker, I’d advise you not to take up any more offers of, ah, free publicity.’

‘I refused to talk about the murder, Inspector!’

‘Am I making myself clear? No radio appearances, no chats to the newspaper, nothing.’

‘I wasn’t planning to.’

‘Is that a yes?’ His gaze hadn’t wavered, and Pippa was starting to feel like a rabbit in headlights.

‘It’s a yes,’ she said.

Inspector Fanshawe glanced at his notebook, and when he looked up the steeliness was gone. ‘Good. We’ll leave it there for today. Interview ends eleven-twenty.’ He switched off the recorder then closed his notebook, and PC Gannet closed his too. 'We may call you back to clarify what you've said, Mrs Parker, or if any new information comes to light. If you think of something which might be helpful to the case, I take it you know to call here.'

Pippa exhaled. 'Yes.'

'Right.' He stood up. 'Oh, and we have your fingerprints on file. Just in case you'd forgotten.'

Pippa scooped up her things and stood. 'I'll let PC Gannet see you out,' said Inspector Fanshawe. 'Goodbye, Mrs Parker. I hope we won't need to meet again.'

Pippa nodded — her brain was too clouded to think of an appropriate response — and walked beside PC Gannet. He remained silent, which was a relief, until they arrived at reception. 'Goodbye, Mrs Parker,' he said, his face expressionless, and Pippa wondered whether that was his training, or whether he was thinking something which he didn't want to give away.

Pippa signed herself out at the desk, pushed open the heavy door, and walked to her car, a small red beacon among the grey and black and silver. She got in, locked the doors, and sat staring through the windscreen at nothing. Half-formed thoughts tangled in her head —

Pippa looked at her hands, gripping the steering wheel at ten to two even though the engine was off.

*Am I a suspect?*

# CHAPTER 12

'I know I said back by one, but it isn't even twelve,' said Sheila, as she opened the door with Ruby balanced on her hip. Then her eyes met Pippa's, and opened wide. 'What's happened?'

'I went to give a statement at the police station,' said Pippa.

'Ohh.' Sheila looked half-curious, half-envious. 'I take it it wasn't a pleasant experience.'

'I feel wrung out,' said Pippa. 'And they said they might call me back in. I'm not sure I can go back in.' She felt her face crumpling, and tried to keep it straight, but it was no good. One sob leaked out, then another. Sheila opened the door wider, and Pippa stumbled inside.

'Now you sit down and have a cry,' said Sheila, leading the way to the lounge. 'I'll get the kettle on and sort out some biscuits. Things always seem better when you have biscuits.' She plopped Ruby into the travel cot which served as a playpen, and scurried to the kitchen.

Pippa perched on the overstuffed sofa and tried to cry quietly and so that Ruby wouldn't see. But Ruby pulled herself to her feet and stretched out a waving hand. 'Ma-ma!'

'Oh Ruby…' Pippa scooped her daughter up and cuddled the warm, wriggly body. Ruby put her thumb in her mouth and gazed up at her mother, then put a fat little hand on Pippa's cheek. Confusion flickered on her face.

'Yes, mummies cry too, sometimes,' said Pippa. 'When people are mean to them.'

'I'm sure they were just doing their job,' said Sheila, coming in with a tray. 'Even if it wasn't very nice for you.'

'I don't mind being questioned,' said Pippa. 'It was the insinuation that made me uncomfortable. They even said they would ring one of my friends to check up on me.'

'At least they told you,' said Sheila, putting the tray down. 'The tea needs another couple of minutes.'

'I'm glad you're so calm about it,' said Pippa. 'I'm not sure whether they think I'm a ghoul or a murderer.'

'You can't be the murderer,' said Sheila. 'Firstly, you're not that sort of person, secondly, you aren't an early riser, and thirdly I doubt you'd have the strength to smash in someone's face if you wanted to. Haven't you read the papers?' She took the tea cosy off the pot and peered in. 'Are you milk in first or afterwards? I can never remember.'

'Afterwards,' said Pippa, kissing Ruby on the top of her head and carrying her back to the cot. 'And no, I haven't been following the case. Partly because everyone's so desperate to get my opinion of it.'

'You should be flattered,' said Sheila, pouring out. 'They think you have insider information.' She put the pot down. 'I do think you could have told me that you were practically there when the body was found.' Her voice sharpened. 'I had to find out from the paper.' She handed Pippa a china cup and saucer.

'The police asked us not to say anything.' It was half-true. 'The news broke the next day, anyway. You didn't miss much.'

'But a *murder*...' Sheila took a Rich Tea from the plate and bit into it without dunking. 'I'm surprised at young Jim Horsley giving you a hard time, when you've given him so much help.' Her lips thinned. 'I've a good mind to pay him a visit at the station.'

'It wasn't Jim Horsley,' said Pippa, selecting a bourbon. 'I had to go to the main station at Gadcester. Inspector Fanshawe and PC Gannet did the interrogation.' She lifted the cup, then stopped. 'Sheila, what did you mean about not being an early riser?'

'Well you aren't, are you dear? Before Freddie came along I'd be lucky to get either of you to answer the telephone before nine in the morning —'

'I meant in relation to the murder?'

'Oh yes.' Sheila looked severe. 'The papers said Tony Green had probably been dead for four hours when he was found. So if he was found just before eleven, he was killed at around seven o'clock.'

'When I was in bed with Simon!'

'I don't need to know about that,' said Sheila. 'But yes.'

Pippa's breath sighed out. 'You don't know how

relieved I am.' She could have hugged Sheila, if Sheila had been that sort of person. 'And the smashing-in?'

Sheila huffed and got up. 'I'll go and fetch the newspapers I've kept. Now that you're paying attention.'

Pippa ate her biscuit, her mood rising with every bite (not that it took her many bites to eat a bourbon, especially when Ruby was watching). Sheila returned with a small pile of newspapers. 'Here we are,' she said, putting them on the coffee table. 'I'll move the tray, and then we can spread out.' She put the tray on the floor, and selected two papers from the pile. Pippa recognised the headlines — she had read them the morning after the murder. 'These don't have much in them, so you can skim if you like. The next few are better, one's got the obituary.'

Pippa discarded the first two and Sheila opened the next one to where she had folded the corner. 'This one's a bit gruesome.'

'Thanks for the warning.' Pippa's eyes ran down the columns.

*...the cause of death was brain injury and bleed caused by several forceful blows to the head, and particularly to the back of the head. The victim was also struck several times in the face, causing a broken nose, a fractured eye socket, and injury to the mouth, as well as cuts, bruising and swelling.*

'Oh, that poor man,' murmured Pippa.

*The variety of injuries, and the difference in their presentation, may mean that more than one weapon was used — and possibly that more than one person was involved.*

*If you think you may have information relating to this, please contact Gadcester Police Station —*

'I hate to disturb you, dear,' said Sheila, 'but it's twenty past twelve.'

'Oh my,' said Pippa. 'Freddie time. Thanks for reminding me.' She closed the paper and got up. 'And thank you for making me feel better. In an odd sort of way.'

'That's quite all right,' said Sheila, rising too, and half-put her arms round Pippa for a moment. 'You'd better pop back for Ruby, you'll never make it otherwise.'

'When I pop back . . . can I borrow the newspapers? I'll look after them.'

Sheila cast her eyes to the ceiling. 'You can, dear. You also *may* borrow the newspapers.' She smiled. 'I was beginning to worry about you.'

***

Pippa ignored the *ping* of her phone as she hurried to the car. Whoever it was could wait. If it was that important, they'd phone. And if it was the police she'd rather ignore it for now, thank you very much.

She knocked on the preschool door at twelve thirty precisely. 'Ah, Mrs Parker,' said Mrs Marks. 'Just in time.'

'Indeed,' said Pippa. 'As usual.'

Freddie ran to Pippa and threw his arms round her. 'Mummy!' he cried. 'I thought you'd forgotten me!' He was the last child there, and Pippa felt a pang of compunction.

'I'm sorry, Fred-Fred,' she said. 'I was talking to Granma Sheila.'

'Where's Ruby?' he asked, frowning and looking for her, as if she might have climbed on the window-ledge or inserted herself in the bookcase.

'At Granma Sheila's. We'll go back for her now.' Pippa led the way to the door. 'Bye, Mrs Marks, must dash!' she called, engineering her departure so as to miss whatever resigned or concerned expression Mrs Marks was wearing. If only it could have been Dawn.

Pippa collected Ruby, her paraphernalia, and a canvas bag of papers from Sheila, and as she strapped Ruby in her phone pinged again. *It had better not be the police,* she thought grimly.

At home Pippa put the bag out of the children's reach and warmed some lovingly pre-prepared chicken and vegetable mush for Ruby, and just as the microwave pinged, her pocket echoed it.

*Not NOW.*

She pulled out the food, stirred it, checked the temperature, and served Ruby, who was waving her plastic spoon as if to an invisible orchestra. 'Let's see how much you can get in your mouth today, Rubes,' she said, sitting next to the high chair and brandishing a spoon of her own.

Ruby giggled and bashed her spoon into the bowl, spattering pale orangey-brown mush over the tray, her bib, and her top. Clearly it was going to be one of those days.

Pippa surrendered when the bowl was two-thirds empty, and considered whether wiping Ruby's face with the bib would make it more or less clean. 'I suppose you want pudding,' she said.

Ruby lifted her arms up. 'Ma-ma!' she proclaimed.

‘Oh no,’ said Pippa. ‘Not until you’re cleaned up.’ She looked at her top, which had suffered in the feeding process. ‘And me.’

She found a jar of chocolate pudding in the cupboard, unscrewed the lid and fetched a fresh spoon. While Ruby feeding herself was of course a worthy goal, she dreaded to think what havoc Ruby could wreak with a spoon and a jar of chocolate pudding —

The doorbell rang. Twice.

Pippa sighed, cast a resigned glance down at herself and walked into the hall.

The doorbell rang twice more. ‘Keep your hair on!’ she shouted, juggling spoon and jar. If it was some random bloke pushing her to let him quote for a resin driveway again —

*What if it’s the police?*

Her hand paused in mid-air.

*Don’t be daft, Pippa,* she told herself. Then, her heart in her mouth, she looked through the glass.

Serendipity was standing outside, and the top of Monty’s smooth brown head was just visible at the bottom of the pane.

Pippa sighed with relief and opened the door. ‘I’m so glad it’s you,’ she said. ‘I thought you were the police.’

Then she saw that Serendipity was trembling. ‘What is it?’

Serendipity didn’t speak, but gazed at Pippa with large tragic eyes. Monty followed suit.

Pippa put the pudding and spoon on the hall table and touched Serendipity’s arm. ‘Come in. Whatever it is, come in.'

'Monty!' Freddie barrelled out of the lounge and embraced the dog heartily.

'I'm sorry,' said Serendipity. 'I tried texting you this morning but you didn't reply —'

'I had my phone on silent,' said Pippa. 'It's a long story.'

'So I tried to text you again but still nothing, so I thought you might be in for lunch —'

'What's wrong?' Pippa took Serendipity through to the dining room. 'Freddie, you can play with Monty in the garden if you promise to be good.'

'Yay!' shouted Freddie, and bounced up and down as Pippa opened the back door.

'Coffee?' Pippa called.

'Thanks, but — you've got your hands full. I just — I thought you should know.'

Pippa shot through to the dining room. Serendipity was sitting in her chair, looking woebegone, while Ruby banged the tray of her highchair with a spoon. 'Know what, Serendipity? What's happened?'

'It probably doesn't sound like much,' said Serendipity, her shoulders relaxing slightly. 'It's the craft demonstration events… I had a message this morning, through my website. It was from someone who'd booked for herself and three friends to come to the Much Gadding demo. She's written to say that she was sorry to cancel at such short notice, but given the recent events they wouldn't feel comfortable attending.'

'Oh,' said Pippa, and an icy finger stroked her throat.

‘If it was just one…’ said Serendipity. ‘The Much Gadding event was almost fully booked. But when I checked on the system, now it’s nearly empty. And some of the other event bookings have gone, too. We’re down to less than half of what we had.’ She looked ready to cry.

‘It’s the murder, isn’t it,’ said Pippa, and it wasn’t a question. ‘People don’t want to come here. I can see why not, right now, but — your events, and the concerts, and all the other things that happen in Much Gadding —’

‘It could be the end of the village,’ whispered Serendipity, blinking back tears.

‘Not if I can help it,’ said Pippa, grimly.

# CHAPTER 13

'I can't see how you'll solve this with a bunch of newspapers,' said Simon, putting a mug of tea down on a coaster. 'Especially at half ten in the evening.'

Pippa slid the coaster further away from the papers covering most of the dining-room table. 'It won't be just newspapers, but it's a start. I can't believe how much I've missed.'

'Well, you have had your nose in a plan for the last fortnight or so.' Simon sat opposite her.

Pippa sighed. 'Just when I thought I had the event stuff sorted out —'

'Some inconsiderate person goes and gets murdered.' Simon nudged her when she didn't respond. 'I am joking.'

'Mm.' Pippa turned a page and scribbled in her notepad. 'I'm trying to make sure we don't end up living in a ghost village.'

'The police can probably handle it by themselves, you know. They do have experience in this sort of thing.'

'Which is why I've solved three cases since we moved here.'

'That was the local police though. Gadcester police probably have better resources.'

'Still the same inspector, though,' said Pippa. 'And if Sheila can pick a hole in their reasoning, well —'

'Oh God,' said Simon. 'The Cagney and Lacey of the shires strike again. I'm going to bed.' He kissed the top of her bent head. 'Make sure you tidy that away before you come up. I know Freddie can't read much yet, but that isn't where I want him to start.'

'Thanks for your enthusiasm,' said Pippa, and turned another page.

***

'Any breakthroughs, Detective?' Simon asked when Pippa climbed into bed.

'Not as yet.' She sighed. 'Maybe I need coffee and doughnuts.'

'Not now you don't, or you'll never sleep.' A brief silence. 'Seriously though, how will you find anything out beyond what's in the papers?'

'I don't know.' That was the problem. She suddenly felt alone, despite Simon's warm presence beside her. It was all very well resolving to find the murderer, bring them to justice and rescue Much Gadding's event industry in the process, but while she had local allies, most of them were little practical use.

'Sleep on it,' said Simon, rubbing her shoulder. 'If you can.' He turned over, and within a few minutes his breathing had settled into the regular rhythm which indicated he was either asleep or heading that way.

Pippa stared at the rectangle of slightly lighter grey which was usually the bedroom window. Someone was out there, someone who had killed and might kill again…

She squeezed her eyes closed and thought of doughnuts, cake, bunting, anything to drive out what had swum into her head.

And she must have succeeded, because when she next opened her eyes the bedroom window was there again, and it was morning.

***

'Penny for them,' said Lila.

'Uh? Oh, sorry.'

'You've been staring at the wall for the last twenty minutes. Are you sure you're OK?' Lila pushed her curls back to reveal a frown. 'You never replied to my text on Saturday, you know.'

'Didn't I?'

'No. I did consider looking through your letterbox in case you were lying dead in the hall.'

'Thanks.' Pippa scanned the room for the children. Freddie was deep in discussion with Henry and Dylan, a toy car clutched in his hand, while Ruby was poking a number-and-letter toy and reacting with delighted surprise every time it flashed or beeped.

'I wondered if you were pretending to be catatonic so no-one asked you about the Ritz Robertson thing.'

'Oh God. I'd nearly forgotten that.'

'What do you mean? It only happened a few days ago.'

'A lot's happened since then. I got grilled at the police

station yesterday.'

'Really?'

'Mm.' Pippa hoped her response would signal to Lila that she didn't want to discuss it.

'Were they pumping you for information?' Lila persisted.

'Excuse me,' said Monika. 'Lila, the rota says that you are serving in the kitchen today, and it is five minutes to eleven.'

'So it is,' said Lila. 'Right with you.' Monika stood waiting while Lila got up. 'Talk later,' she said, turning to Pippa and rolling her eyes. Pippa smiled sympathetically, but was quite glad that Monika watched Lila all the way to the kitchen.

As it turned out, they didn't talk later. Imogen buttonholed Pippa in the snack queue, with the opener 'So, Much Gadding Primary…' The parents' ears pricked up as if they were a pack of dogs who had heard the word *walkies*, and the resulting conversation was lively enough to get them through the queue, the consumption of drinks and snacks, and to putting-away time.

'There's an open morning at Upper Gadding Primary on Friday,' said Sam. 'Had you thought of there?'

'Not really,' said Pippa. 'We're not particularly religious.'

'Oh but it's Church of England, you don't have to be. I mean, they don't ask for a reference from the parish priest. Not like some of the Catholic schools.' Pippa wondered how much time Sam had spent going through the schools booklet. 'And it's fairly easy to get to.'

'D'you mind if I come?' asked Imogen. 'I could drive us if you want.'

'Yes, we could car share,' said Caitlin. 'Like a group outing!'

'Mrs Marks'll wonder where we've all gone,' said Sam, grinning. 'We'd better warn her!' And the excited buzz continued. Pippa wasn't sure if it was group hysteria at the school situation, or a feeling of safety in numbers. At any rate she'd have something to compare Much Gadding with. Perhaps it would be a good back-up, or even a first choice. *At least it'll take my mind off everything else*. She caught sight of Lila, looking at her a little oddly from across the room, and smiled back. Lila was probably just worried about her, like a good friend.

***

However, back at home for lunch, Pippa had a new mystery to solve. 'I literally don't know where it all goes,' she said, upending the plastic milk bottle to get the last trickle into her tea. Even so, a hardened builder would probably have pronounced it a bit on the strong side.

Pippa sighed. She did know where it all went — Freddie's cereal and glasses of milk ate through the supply. And both children got through inordinate amounts of toast. She opened the lid of the bread bin with a sinking feeling. Two slices left.

'We bought a loaf at the weekend!' she wailed. 'Come on, you two, we're walking to the shop.'

'*Ohhhh.*' Freddie wrenched himself from the screen with an anguished expression on his face. 'Can't we go when *SuperMouse* has finished?'

‘Not if Mummy’s going to have tea with milk. And not if you’re going to have beans on toast.’

Ruby clapped her hands together and beamed. ‘Bee-do-doh!’ she crowed.

‘Exactly. Shoes on, Freddie.’

Once the children had been mobilised, Pippa advanced on the country store at a brisk pace. While the day had started out sunny, dark clouds loomed over the Hall, and the last thing she wanted was for them to get caught in a rain shower. Freddie would never let her hear the end of it. She swung the pushchair round and opened the shop door with her free hand, preparatory to backing up the step —

‘Hello.’

Pippa jumped. Standing on the pavement was PC Horsley. ‘Oh, er, hello.’

‘Do you want me to get the door?’ he asked.

‘No, no it’s fine,’ she said, and reversed in. It felt oddly formal, as if she were departing from the Queen’s presence. The policeman held the door anyway, and followed her in.

The store seemed much as usual, smelling of sawdust, and with much of its produce laid out in plastic trays — seed balls, dog chews, pig’s ears… Pippa steered past those and went to the refrigerated cabinet where the milk lived. And yet something was different. PC Horsley’s presence in the shop made her feel slightly wary.

‘Hello, Freddie,’ he said. ‘How are you today?’

‘Mummy wouldn’t let me watch the end of *SuperMouse*,’ said Freddie, pouting.

‘Oh dear,’ said Jim Horsley. ‘Do I need to arrest her?’

'Yayyyy!' said Freddie. 'Have you got handcuffs?'

'I'm afraid I left those at the station.'

Pippa took out a four-pint container and closed the cabinet door with a satisfying thunk. 'If you didn't keep stealing all the milk, we wouldn't have to come out for emergency supplies, would we?'

'Your mother has a point,' PC Horsley told Freddie. 'Maybe I should arrest you too.' Freddie backed away hurriedly.

The policeman crossed to the cabinet and got a pint of milk, and then Pippa understood what was — not wrong, but unusual. She had never seen PC Horsley doing non-crime-related things before.

'Do you know,' she said, conversationally, 'I don't think I've ever seen you off-duty. I mean, I know you're in uniform, but —'

'Mm,' said PC Horsley, in a way which reminded her of her own *Mm* to Lila. He went to the counter.

'That'll be sixty-five pence, officer,' said the brown-coated shopkeeper.

PC Horsley rummaged in his pocket.

'Can I interest you in any of our special offers today, sir? Twenty percent off birdseed, flea collars two for one?'

PC Horsley put a pound on the counter, and the shopkeeper laid his finger on it. 'For the rest of that pound I could throw in a squeaky toy.'

'I'll pass, thanks,' said the policeman.

The shopkeeper sighed. 'Your loss,' he said, picking out an assortment of small change and lining it up as if it were about to face the firing squad.

Pippa picked up a wholemeal sliced and approached the stand-off. 'Just these, please,' she said, putting the milk and bread on the edge of the counter.

'Two pounds seventy,' the shopkeeper said, wearily. 'I won't bother asking.'

Pippa found the right money, put it down, and left. The bell clanged, and again PC Horsley was behind her, holding the door. 'Thanks,' she said. 'Um, are you going straight back to the station?'

'I'm on a break,' said PC Horsley. 'Would the children like to play on the green for a few minutes?'

The clouds' threats were still, so far, empty ones. Pippa gave Freddie a slice of bread for duck-feeding, popped Ruby on the grass, and sat down at one end of the bench. PC Horsley took the other end, and Pippa waited.

'I imagine you've noticed something,' he said.

Pippa looked across. He was watching a mallard drift over the pond. 'Just now, or earlier?'

'Earlier,' he said.

'I got called into Gadcester police station yesterday to give a statement,' said Pippa.

Now PC Horsley was looking at her. 'Inspector Fanshawe?'

'Yes, and PC Gannet.'

'How was it? If you don't mind me asking,' he added quickly.

'Honestly? Uncomfortable.' She wondered whether to say the thing on the tip of her tongue. *Oh, to heck with it.* 'They pretty much told me to keep my nose out.'

'Did they.' He was back to watching the duck. 'Seems

to be a habit of theirs.'

'Are you OK with that?'

'No.' He picked a speck from his jumper and flicked it away. 'It happened here. It should be investigated here, not at arm's length.'

'I'm sure it's nothing to do with your capabilities,' said Pippa. 'They probably have better facilities at Gadcester. It's a big station.'

'It's a big case,' said Jim Horsley. 'Gadcester police think they can handle it better than a lone policeman in a concrete shoebox. But that isn't the only reason. They want to close more small stations. Cuts, you know. Efficiencies. And we're one of the stations they're looking at.'

'You're kidding.' Pippa stared at him, open-mouthed.

'Wish I was.'

'Then there's another reason to get on and find the murderer.'

'Excuse me?' Now it was Jim Horsley's turn to stare.

'The police station's in danger, local businesses are in danger, and while there's a murderer on the loose, we could be in danger. It's time we took matters into our own hands.' Pippa nodded decisively, and out of the corner of her eye saw Ruby crawling in the direction of the duck pond. 'Don't you agree?' she called over her shoulder, as she rushed to scoop up her errant daughter.

And when she turned back, PC Horsley was smiling.

# CHAPTER 14

'Bye, Freddie!' Pippa called, as the preschool door clicked shut. Then she turned Ruby's pushchair and strolled to the main road. *Cross over, then walk either into the village or home. Just as usual.*

Pippa walked alongside the village green, past the row of cottages with a blue plaque commemorating Clementina Stoate (she really must read her poems one day), and down towards St Saviour's church hall, where playgroup was held.

Except that it was Wednesday, and playgroup didn't happen on a Wednesday.

She walked along the concrete path anyway, then skirted the hall on its right-hand side. The churchyard wall was on her right, and beyond it was a scrubby area of uncut grass and weeds. Pippa wheeled Ruby through the grass, hoping there weren't any hidden thistles or nettles, until she came to a square pebble-dashed wall with a white-painted back door just off centre. She tapped, and the door opened immediately.

'In you come,' said Jim Horsley. 'No-one saw you, did they?'

'I doubt it,' said Pippa. 'The village is pretty dead at this time, and on Wednesday mornings there's a lull between the early slimmers and the eleven o'clock Zumba crew.'

'OK, but be careful. The last thing we need is people noticing things and asking questions.'

'Well, no,' said Pippa. 'That's our job.'

'Quite.' PC Horsley led the way down the corridor into the back room, walked to the kitchen area, and flicked the kettle on.

'I don't suppose you've got any doughnuts in?' said Pippa. 'Just asking.'

'How long have you got?' he asked, getting two mugs from the cupboard. 'It's milk no sugar, isn't it?'

'That's right.' Pippa watched him slam-dunk teabags into the mugs. 'I have to be at preschool for half twelve, but if Ruby gets restless you may want me out long before that.'

Ruby chuckled and squeaked. 'Come on, let's get you set up,' said Pippa, unfolding her play gym and spreading it on the carpet, and placing Ruby's activity centre within reach. 'There.' She unbuckled Ruby and lifted her out of the chair, and a smell wafted upwards. 'Ooh, we need to make a pitstop. Is there a bathroom we can use?'

'There is, but it's tiny,' said PC Horsley. 'You might be better doing it here.'

'Fair enough,' said Pippa, and reached for her changing

bag.

Three minutes later Ruby was clean and bashing away happily, while Pippa and PC Horsley sat opposite each other at the table.

'I won't be able to share anything confidential with you,' said PC Horsley. 'That's more than my job is worth. In fact, I'd probably go straight to jail. Do not pass go, do not collect two hundred pounds.'

'Understood,' said Pippa. 'So what *can* we do?'

'Bounce ideas off each other. Come up with theories. Go and ask questions.' Jim Horsley raised his eyebrows. 'Will that do?'

'Oh God, yes,' said Pippa.

'So, how far have you got?' he asked, and Pippa reached for her notepad.

'From the info in the papers, Tony Green was killed at about seven o'clock,' she said. 'I can't claim credit for that, my mother-in-law worked it out.'

PC Horsley grunted. 'I only have room for one unofficial co-investigator,' he said.

'I can't see Sheila sneaking round to the back so you're probably safe,' said Pippa. 'She'd expect to be blue-lighted to Gadcester station.'

'Quite. Did you notice much about the immediate surroundings when you came to the meadow?'

Pippa frowned. 'Long grass, flattened where the — where the body was, obviously. And a bit beyond.'

'Yes. There was a line of flattened grass from a mown path maybe twenty feet away, leading to where the body was found.'

'So the body was dragged from there.'

'Mm. Did you think the body was well-hidden?' PC Horsley studied her speculatively.

'Not particularly. I mean, it was deep in the meadow, but with the path nearby it was only a matter of time before someone found it.'

'Yes. Could they have hidden it better?'

'They could have dragged the body further from the path. Unless they didn't have time, or they weren't strong enough. Although anyone who could kill someone like that sounds pretty strong to me.'

'Yeeeees. But it probably means it was just one person, because two could easily have shifted the body. They could even have dumped it in the river.'

'Ugh.' A particularly loud bash from Ruby made Pippa look across. 'I'm glad you're having fun,' she said severely. Ruby giggled and rolled over.

'And you're not?' asked PC Horsley, glancing at her untouched mug of tea.

'Hating every minute,' said Pippa. 'Carry on.'

'So one person — unless there was more than one, and one left the other to hide the body, which makes no sense.'

'No. And it feels like a one-person sort of crime.'

Jim Horsley's eyebrows lifted.

'Would you want to smash someone up like that in front of a witness?' Pippa saw the policeman's eyes shift to a point behind her, and turned to see her daughter crawling towards the door. 'Oh no you don't,' she said, scooping Ruby up and sitting her on her lap.

'You have some interesting perspectives, Mrs Parker,'

said the policeman, with a gleam in his eye. 'Embarrassment as a cause of lone crime.'

'It was vicious, though. From what I've read,' said Pippa, restraining a squirming Ruby.

'It was.' PC Horsley swigged from his mug. 'Which probably means there was a motive. It wasn't a random attack.'

'Not unless the attacker was insane,' said Pippa. 'I mean, to go and lie in wait in the dark for someone and then bash them like that . . . you'd have to have a reason.'

'You'd think so,' mused PC Horsley. 'So a motive. But what was Tony Green doing at the meadow so early? A survey of dog walkers, perhaps?'

'He could have been thinking about the houses, or taking an early morning stroll,' said Pippa. 'He did seem like the sort of person who might do that, from what I've seen and what Simon said —'

PC Horsley's mug froze in mid-air. 'Simon? Your husband Simon?'

'That's the one,' said Pippa. 'Tony Green was a few years above him at high school.' Ruby bucked like a horse and Pippa let her slide to the floor where she stood on tiptoe, holding on to Pippa's fingers. 'Come on then, Ruby, walk with me.'

'Interview him,' said PC Horsley, setting his mug precisely in the middle of the coaster. 'Interview him and take notes. Whatever he can remember will help us.'

'Sir yes sir.' Pippa clicked her heels and PC Horsley glared at her. 'Sorry, but you just went a bit, um, authoritative.'

'It does go with the job, Pippa,' PC Horsley observed. 'Anyway, the weapon.'

'Yes,' said Pippa, walking backwards carefully while Ruby giggled and swayed like a falling tree. 'Any leads on that? I only know what I've read in the paper, and that said a heavy object, probably with an edge. And no, I don't want to see the pictures.'

'I'm not going to show you,' said the policeman. 'That's the last thing you want in your head. I wish I hadn't seen it.'

'I'm sorry,' said Pippa.

He shrugged. 'It's my job. I don't have any insider info, nothing except what's in the papers. The Inspector's keeping it close to his chest, and young Gannet's no better.'

'He probably thinks this is his big break,' said Pippa, remembering PC Gannet's official manner.

'It doesn't work like that,' said PC Horsley. 'You don't get promoted for solving a big case.'

'Yeah, anyway,' said Pippa, a little sourly, reaching the door and turning Ruby round. 'The weapon.'

'Mm.' PC Horsley tapped his pen on the desk. 'A heavy object, or certainly one with a bit of weight. Not a sharp object, though. There were no stab wounds, and not many cuts. It was all about force.'

Pippa thought. 'So a blunt instrument. A cosh, maybe?' She remembered her first case, and shuddered. Ruby wobbled, and squeaked.

'But the papers said that the object had an edge,' PC Horsley replied. 'And that's consistent with what I saw.'

'A spade? That could work, and it isn't a particularly

suspicious item. Or maybe a trowel? That would be easier to hide — although it would have to be a pretty strong one.'

'True. Plus it's something lots of people have.' PC Horsley scribbled in his notebook.

'There are those allotments further along the road, past the ford,' said Pippa. 'You could maybe put up a notice on the gate, ask if anyone's had tools go missing.'

'What a good idea.' And for the first time since her arrival, PC Horsley cracked a smile.

***

Ruby let the grown-ups have their fun for a few more minutes before plopping to the floor and letting out an ear-piercing shriek. Pippa leaned down to pick her up and Ruby immediately giggled and grabbed her hair.

'Someone's had enough,' said Pippa. 'To be honest, I'm amazed we got as long as we did.'

'So am I.' PC Horsley got up and came over. He tickled Ruby under the chin, which made her let go of Pippa's hair. 'Have my finger instead, Ruby, much less painful.'

'You may regret that,' said Pippa. 'She's got the grip of a boa constrictor.'

'Has she, now,' said PC Horsley. 'Wonder where she gets that from.' His mouth twitched.

'I'll take that as a compliment,' said Pippa.

'When could you come again?' PC Horsley looked almost shy. 'I thought we got a lot done, considering.'

'Well, on Monday morning I'm actually child-free, although I am supposed to be working.' Pippa considered. 'But as my business appears to be drying up thanks to the murderer, I guess you could call this business activity.'

'OK.' Jim Horsley uncurled Ruby's fingers from his own very gently, and Pippa tried not to think about how close he was, or watch his square-tipped fingers handling Ruby's chubby little digits. 'Mondays are usually quiet, so if you could interview your husband before then, and report back, that would be useful.'

'Simon, yes,' said Pippa, stepping back to increase the distance between Ruby and PC Horsley's finger — and also between PC Horsley and herself. 'I'll do my best. And I'll spend some time thinking about it all.'

'So shall I,' said the policeman. 'Do you need help packing up?'

'If you could fold up the mat, and put it in the bag…' Pippa proceeded to issue directions while PC Horsley crouched at her feet and folded the mat every which way but the right one. 'No, it doesn't make logical sense, but that's the way it works.'

'Sounds like most things,' said PC Horsley, wrestling the folded mat into the bag and zipping it closed. 'Anyway.' He held the door for Pippa, then followed her to the pushchair, which was blocking the exit. He stepped over it, opened the door, and peered out. 'Seems quiet.' He pulled it to, then watched Pippa put the flailing Ruby into her chariot. 'Till next time, Pippa.'

'Yes.' Pippa snapped Ruby's harness together. 'Till next time, Constable Horsley.'

His eyes crinkled. 'I also answer to Jim.'

'Um, yes. Of course. Well, till next time, um, Jim.'

PC Horsley stepped out to let her get by, then beat a

hasty retreat, closing the door behind him. Pippa looked at the blank white door for a moment, then made her way back to the road, on the alert for potential snoopers. As far as she could tell there was no-one *to* snoop, but you never knew.

She hesitated by the green, and checked her watch. Half past eleven. She could make the most of an extra hour in the village. Take Ruby for a snack in the tearoom, or get books from the library… But no. She felt jumpy, full of static, likely to get an electric shock if she touched anything.

Or maybe it was the other way round —

*For heaven's sake, Pippa, you aren't fifteen,* she told herself. She turned the pushchair and walked home, hoping her face wasn't as pink as it felt.

# CHAPTER 15

'You aren't going to choir?' Simon stared at her, then snorted. 'Typical. I actually remembered and came home on time, so of course you aren't going.'

'Sorry,' muttered Pippa.

'Anyway, why not?' Simon worked his tie from side to side, pulling it loose as if it were strangling him. 'Fancied a quiet evening in with the love of your life?'

'In a manner of speaking, yes,' said Pippa. 'I've already fed the children.'

'Wow, you *are* serious.' He grinned and dropped the looped tie over her head, then tugged gently on the loose end.

'Simon…' Pippa resisted the urge to step into his arms. 'I wanted to ask you about Tony Green. When you were at school together.'

'Oh.' Simon made a face. 'Just when I thought I was getting somewhere. But why tonight?'

'Well…' Pippa leaned forward to murmur in his ear,

even though the children were engrossed in *SuperMouse*. 'You can't tell anyone, but I went to see PC Horsley this morning…'

*Who also answers to Jim.*

'…and he thought that as you knew Tony Green years ago you might remember something useful.'

'I didn't know him well,' said Simon. 'I knew *of* him, but that isn't the same thing at all. Everyone in school knew Stinky Green —'

'Please don't call him that.'

'But everyone did,' said Simon. 'There's something for you. I don't think he minded though. He was an easy-going sort of kid.'

'There. We're getting somewhere,' said Pippa. 'Anyway, can we wait till the kids are in bed? I want to take notes.'

'Sure,' said Simon. 'What's for dinner?'

***

Another reason for doing the interview tonight, and missing choir, was that Pippa had been on the go since leaving the police station. Ruby, perhaps basking in Pippa's undivided attention, had refused to be put down, requiring endless games of peek-a-boo, knee bounces, and songs, until it was time to return to preschool. Freddie had been no better. Today's preschool activity had been making collages, and it was fair to say that he had been bitten by the bug. Two hours, several magazines, a glue stick and a raft of craft supplies later, Pippa had achieved nothing but cutting out pictures of cars, trees and houses, which Freddie arranged in various combinations, considered briefly, then rejected. 'I'm bored,' he announced, pushing the paper away. 'Can we go to the park?'

'You could watch a film,' said Pippa, hopefully, then felt a pang of guilt that she was encouraging screen time rather than embracing healthy outdoor activities. 'No, of course we'll go to the park.' That was another hour gone. The worst of it was that with the constant requirement to cut pictures out and retrieve the dropped glue stick and push the children on the swings and activate the roundabout, there was no room in Pippa's mind to do any serious thinking. What there was room for, though, was the disturbing, yet at the same time pleasing memory of working more closely with Jim Horsley. *I wonder how old he is*, she thought, then gave herself a mental slap on the wrist. *He's not even particularly attractive. Unless you like that whole man-in-uniform thing. I wonder what he looks like out of it — NO! NO! I mean in normal clothes!* And a silent barrage of self-recrimination followed.

So in a way, telling Simon that she had been to see PC Horsley was a relief. She wasn't keeping it a secret from her husband; it was purely a business matter. And because it was purely a business matter, she was making Simon's favourite dinner of steak and chips.

'That was very nice,' said Simon, putting his knife and fork together on his plate. 'Why do I get the feeling I'm being buttered up?'

'Can't I make you a nice dinner without you thinking I'm up to something?' Pippa sawed a chip in half with her steak knife, eyes on her plate.

'On a week night, when the kids have probably been running you ragged? And when it means you're missing choir practice?' Simon grinned. 'No, you can't. Come on Pip, what's going on?'

'Nothing's going on.' Pippa picked up the plates and took them to the kitchen. Thin streams of watery blood ran under the cutlery, and she rinsed the plates before sliding them into the dishwasher and closing the door on them. She paused for a moment to clear her head. Nothing *was* going on and she wasn't doing anything she shouldn't be. She was helping the police with their enquiries. Even if they weren't the police assigned to the case. Now Jim Horsley might be doing something wrong . . . but that wasn't her business, was it?

Pippa washed her hands at the kitchen tap, dried them on the scrubby towel she always meant to replace, and returned to the dining room. Her notebook was waiting on the sideboard.

Simon had poured more wine while she was clearing away. 'I take it that means there isn't any pudding,' he said, eyeing the notebook.

Pippa raised her eyebrows. 'Do you want pudding?'

'A chat about the day would be nice,' he said. Then he sighed. 'Go on, start the interrogation. Although I have no idea what you or the police think I know.'

Pippa wrote the date and *Interview with Simon Parker* at the top of a new page, and underlined it. 'OK.' She took a deep breath. 'How long did you know Tony Green?'

Simon thought. 'He was, what, three years above me at school. I don't remember him at primary school much, except that he was one of the big kids. You know how the kids in the top class seem years older and twice your size?'

Pippa nodded.

'I remember him better at GadMag, but of course he left after GCSEs, so that was only a couple of years.'

'But you do remember him.'

'Yeah. He stuck out, kind of. His hair was different from the other lads, longer, scruffier. His shirt was always hanging out. I mean, most of us had our shirts out some of the time, but his was always like that. I think the teachers had stopped bothering to tell him to tuck it in.' Simon frowned as he sipped his wine, then his eyebrows unknitted. 'I know who he reminded me of. Not when he grew up, but when he was in school. You know Scooby Doo? Not the films, the old cartoon.'

'I know Scooby Doo,' said Pippa, wondering if Inspector Fanshawe or PC Horsley had situations like this when they interviewed people, and if so, how they dealt with them.

'He was like Shaggy. The other characters are all just regular, neat and tidy, and then there's Shaggy with his long hair and his baggy clothes and he doesn't fit in. Looking back, I don't think Tony fitted in. He always seemed to be on his own. His name was never read out in assembly, he wasn't on any teams.'

Pippa wrote busily as Simon spoke. 'Did you ever speak to him?'

Simon snorted. 'No. Year 7s don't speak to year 10s. But he spoke to me, once. I was sitting with a friend on the school field — can't remember why, we usually played football — and he came and had a go at me for pulling up daisies. I mean, a proper rant. I hadn't even realised I was doing it. I didn't know what to say so I didn't say anything, and he just muttered about mindless vandalism and the planet, and then wandered off.'

'And that was it?'

'That was it. He didn't come back for A-levels. The next time I heard anything about him was through the school e-newsletter a couple of years ago. They invited him to speak at prize-giving day.'

'Before we moved here, then.'

'Yes, in the summer.'

'I don't suppose you've still got a copy of the newsletter…'

'Doubt it, I usually delete them once I've flicked through. It's probably somewhere on the school website.'

'Thanks.' Pippa picked up her phone and opened the browser, then realised the laptop would probably work better and looked round for it. *Ah, in its bag for once*. She got up.

'Does that mean I'm free to go, your honour?' Simon asked.

Pippa looked up. 'Sorry. Yes, of course you are.' He was smiling, but there was something behind the smile. 'You can go and watch rubbish if you like. Do you want a cup of tea? I can make you one.'

'Why do I think I'm being got rid of?' He sat at the table, twisting the stem of his wineglass. The base of the glass scraped on the coaster, setting Pippa's teeth on edge.

'I want to try and find the newsletter while it's fresh in my mind,' she said, putting the laptop on the table and opening the lid.

‘Mmm.’ Simon was showing no signs of moving. ‘I still don’t see why it’s so urgent, though.’

‘It isn’t, exactly.’ Pippa typed *Gadding Magna High newsletter* into the search engine, and clicked on the third result that came up. The GadMag website came up, with a list of newsletters, and she scrolled down to 2015. Prize-giving would be in July, surely…

‘Pippa. I’m still here.’ His smile had disappeared. ‘What is so urgent that you’re working on this at nine o’clock in the evening? Do you think Jim Horsley’s sitting at his computer right now?’

‘He might be.’ Pippa had a vision of Jim Horsley sitting in front of a computer screen in a dimly-lit room, still in uniform but with his cap off, his face illuminated in a moody glow by strings of scrolling data. OK, the police station actually had fluorescent strip lights, but anyway… The pair of them working, while everyone else was asleep. And not being difficult and asking awkward questions.

Simon snorted. ‘I doubt it.’

‘And even if he isn’t, PC Horsley has all day to investigate stuff. I don’t.’

‘Exactly. He’s paid to do this, and you aren’t.’ Simon looked at his watch. ‘Since you clearly don’t want to be bothered with my company, I’m going out to the pub.’

‘It isn’t like that —’ But Simon was already in the hall, unhooking his jacket. The front door shut a little more loudly than it needed to.

Pippa sighed and poured herself another half-glass of wine before returning to her perusal of the newsletter. There was a photo of Tony Green giving his speech, looking like Lord of the Rings man rather than Shaggy from Scooby Doo. His shirt was still untucked, but it was clean, ironed, and teamed with smart trousers. She read the text below.

*Former pupil Tony Green (1992-97), Chief Executive of Green Construction, gave a rousing speech where he urged pupils to follow their hearts to establish a successful career. Mr Green, who has built his business on environmentally-friendly solutions to housing problems, hopes to develop a carbon-neutral estate in his former home village, Much Gadding.*

Pippa tapped her teeth with a pen as she reread the text. Anyone who had attended the prize-giving, or read the newsletter afterwards, would know that Tony Green was planning to build in Much Gadding. She peered at the photos, but the attendees were small blurs of pattern and colour. The article referred to *pupils, parents and members of the local community*, which was annoyingly vague. Still, it was a lead of sorts. She bookmarked the newsletter page, closed the laptop, and drank the dregs of her wine. Bed was calling.

Pippa was drifting into sleep when she heard Simon's key. There was a pause before the front door closed, quietly this time. The subdued clatter of his keys on the hall table, another pause, then running water in the kitchen. How long had he been out? She glanced at the clock: *11.05*.

He came upstairs a few minutes later and Pippa considered saying hello, then remembered that he had walked out in a huff and decided not to. Let him apologise.

She waited, in the darkness. Running water again, in the bathroom, and toothbrush noises.

Eventually he came back in, and she heard his watch on the bedside table, coins clinking, clothes falling to the floor. Then he spoke, low. 'I can't tell if you're awake, Pippa. But if you are, I am *so* annoyed with you.' The bed dipped on his side, and the duvet pulled away from her slightly as Simon settled himself, but he stayed firmly on his side.

Pippa stared into the darkness. Whatever it was, there was no point having a row in the middle of the night. But she wasn't sure she wanted tomorrow to come, either. She closed her eyes, briefly saw Jim Horsley in his illuminated data stream, and switched him off.

# CHAPTER 16

Pippa awoke to find herself on the extreme edge of the bed. She didn't remember moving there, so she could only assume it was a subconscious retreat from anticipated bother.

'Oh, so you've decided to wake up at last,' Simon commented as soon as she moved. He had clearly been waiting for a sign of life, ready to recommence hostilities.

Pippa dragged herself to a sitting position and eyed her bedside table. There was no mug of tea on it.

'That's how angry I am,' said Simon.

Pippa folded her arms and glared. 'Are you going to tell me what you're so angry about, or am I supposed to guess?'

'Oh, I'll tell you.' Simon drank from his own mug — *so he deliberately didn't make me a drink,* fumed Pippa — and set it down with a sharp clack. 'When I went to the pub last night, one of the two old boys who sit in the corner came up to me at the bar. "Saw your missus this morning in the village," he said.'

'Well, so what?' said Pippa, with a rising feeling of dread.

'He nudged me,' Simon snapped. 'He bloody nudged me and said "Saw her coming out from the wasteland round the back of the church looking proper furtive." And then he winked and said "Thought you should know before you get it from someone else." If he hadn't been so old I'd have punched him.'

'Oh,' said Pippa. 'I wasn't being furtive.'

'Yes you bloody were!' said Simon. 'Why else would you be messing around behind the church?'

'I had Ruby with me!' cried Pippa.

'That's never stopped you doing anything!' Simon countered. 'And I bet you never considered what people might think!'

'What do you mean, what people might think? Why was he even watching?'

'Because the old codger's got nothing better to do. As for what people might think — what do people usually think when they see a woman sneaking about looking furtive?'

'Oh,' said Pippa, feeling her whole face burn as if someone had put the sun next to her and switched it on. 'I promise it wasn't that.'

'I figured,' Simon retorted. 'If it was anyone else I'd probably have thought the same as the old man, but with you — Let's face it, you're far more likely to be snooping after a crime.'

'I went to see PC Horsley, but it seemed wiser to go

round the back,' Pippa gabbled.

'I hope that isn't a euphemism,' Simon remarked, and she couldn't tell from his expression whether it was a joke or not.

'There's nothing going on,' she said, to be on the safe side. 'It's just that he isn't officially on the case.'

'Maybe not,' said Simon. 'But be careful, Pippa. You know what people in the village can be like, and if they think you're up to something —'

'Which I'm *not*,' said Pippa, firmly.

'If they think you're up to something, they won't hesitate to share it.'

'All right,' said Pippa. 'I'll bear it in mind. No more furtive behaviour.' She sighed, relieved that by venting his anger, Simon appeared to have dispelled it.

'Thank you.' Simon leaned across and kissed her on the mouth. 'Oh, and I found out the answer to one of the questions I asked you last night,' he murmured.

'Did you?' said Pippa, kissing him back. 'Which one?'

'The one about Jim Horsley.'

She hoped Simon hadn't noticed the little start she gave. 'I think I've forgotten.'

'Whether he'd still be at work at nine in the evening. He was in the pub when I got there, with his girlfriend. Well, I assume she is, I've seen them in there before.'

'Yeah, probably,' said Pippa, trying to keep her voice light.

'You mean you don't know?' Simon laughed. 'Some detective you are. Right, shower time.'

Pippa considered mentioning tea, but on balance, she

didn't think she deserved it.

***

*Ah, the sanctuary of playgroup*, thought Pippa, as she wheeled Ruby up to the church hall with Freddie at her side, sticking to the centre of the path and looking as unfurtive as she possibly could. She was early, but as it was her turn to put the toys out she hoped no random snooper would hold that against her.

As she rummaged in her bag for the large iron key Pippa heard steps approaching, accompanied by a complaining voice. 'Why are we going so fast, Mummy?' Lila, in her Thursday work uniform of wide-legged trousers, silk shirt and ballet pumps, was towing her daughter up the path. Bella looked much the same as usual, only a shade more mutinous.

'Hi Lila,' said Pippa, turning back to the door. 'Just opening up.'

'I can see that,' said Lila, in a tone which made Pippa look at her again. She detected approaching thunder, possibly with a side order of rain, but she had no idea why.

'Let me get toys out for the kids,' she said, as she opened the door.

Silently Lila helped her move the big plastic kitchen to its usual spot. Pippa rolled out the mat, and put the garage on top, plus some smaller toys to keep Ruby occupied. 'What is it?' she said in an undertone, stepping towards the toy cupboard.

'Why are you avoiding me?' Lila asked, point-blank.

'I'm not avoiding you,' said Pippa. 'Can you keep it down a bit?' She shot a glance at the children, who were paying them no attention whatsoever.

'I don't want to keep it down a bit!' Lila said, louder. 'I want to know!'

'For heaven's sake, Lila, the kids have been antsy all morning and I was hoping for a break. What do you want to know?'

'Why you won't talk to me. Ever since Jeff and Simon went for a drink together you've been off with me. You don't answer texts, *you* don't text, and you don't talk to me at playgroup, apart from hello.'

'I talked to you on Tuesday!'

'Yeah, for thirty seconds.'

'It wasn't my fault Monika came to get you.'

'No, but afterwards you went and talked to the others about school stuff.'

'Well, yes. It's important.'

'And I'm not.' Lila's lower lip moved forward a little, and she looked uncannily like Bella for a moment.

'People will be arriving any minute,' said Pippa, in what she felt was a very reasonable manner.

'I don't care.' The lip trembled.

'Maybe I do.' Pippa took Lila's arm and pulled her into the cupboard. 'I have no idea why you're cross with me. Spill.'

'Jeff's been a bit distant with me ever since he went for that drink with your husband,' muttered Lila, shaking her off. 'And so have you. I don't know what was said, but I'm guessing it isn't good. And if I have you two to thank…' Her hands began to clench, then seemed to remember where they were, and relaxed. 'Fine, then don't be my friend. I've got other friends.' She walked out of the cupboard, then pulled a plastic chair from the stack in the corner and flung herself into it, the utter embodiment of sulkiness.

Pippa huffed, went and got her own chair, and put it beside Lila's. 'I didn't know Simon and Jeff had gone for a pint together till he came back. All I do know is that they got on and they talked about stuff.'

Lila's head swivelled round. 'Me stuff?'

Now Pippa understood Simon's exasperation. 'Just stuff, he said. I haven't put him up to anything, and the only reason I haven't texted as much as usual is that I've been quite busy. If you hadn't noticed.'

Lila said nothing.

'Fine, I've said my piece and you can think what you like.' Pippa stood up.

'Wait,' said Lila. 'You mean Simon didn't tell you what they talked about?'

'Well, no,' said Pippa. 'I think it was what he'd call a man-to-man conversation. They probably didn't even mention you.'

'Oh.' Lila stared into the distance. 'I thought he'd have said.'

'Has Jeff been distant?' Pippa asked.

'I'm not sure,' said Lila, frowning.

'Oh I give up. Maybe you should just talk to him.'

'Like you do with Simon?' said Lila, pointedly. But she was half-smiling.

Ruby, perhaps sensing the easing tension, decided to ramp it back up, throwing her rattle and shrieking for it to be returned to her.

'Shut up and make yourself useful, Lila.' Pippa pointed to the toy cupboard, retrieved the rattle, and sat Ruby on her lap. 'What a fuss over nothing,' she said, ostensibly to her daughter.

***

By the time playgroup came to an end, Pippa really did crave sanctuary. All the mums who were attending the Upper Gadding Primary open morning the next day were as high as kites, as if they were going on some kind of group jolly. An educational group jolly, no less. Pippa, on her knees helping Ruby to build a tower of blocks, could hear shrieks and giggles from the chairs behind her at increasingly regular intervals. Was it too late to invent a forgotten prior engagement? But she had offered to take Imogen and Henry. *Darn.* There was nothing for it.

But the school outing wasn't till tomorrow, and now she *needed* peace and quiet, even if only for a few minutes. She packed up the children bang on time and waited outside for the others to get themselves together and leave, since she was the key-holder. And this was one of the days when she wished she wasn't.

'Why have we come out so early, Mummy?' whined Freddie, trailing the toe of his shoe along the path.

'Don't do that, you'll scuff your shoe,' said Pippa automatically. 'We aren't early, everyone else is a bit late.'

'Mummy says you're late, Livvy,' Freddie observed gleefully when she opened the door. Livvy gazed up at Pippa, half-puzzled, half-frightened.

'No I didn't.'

'You did!' Freddie said, with an accusing glare. Sam, following her daughter out, raised her eyebrows.

'I didn't mean it like that,' Pippa said, feeling herself to be on shaky ground. 'We'll wait over there and give people room.'

She wheeled Ruby off the path, then remembered her conversation with Simon and wheeled her back onto it. She couldn't decide whether her movements were furtive or unhinged. Freddie followed, muttering 'You *did* say everyone was late,' not quite under his breath.

Once the hall was finally empty and locked, Pippa set off to the library. It would probably be a brief respite, but better than nothing.

'Where are we going?' Freddie asked suspiciously.

'To the library,' said Pippa. 'You can choose some books, and then maybe we can read them together this afternoon.' That was the sort of thing she ought to be able to say to a teacher tomorrow morning. Pippa imagined herself smiling in a got-it-together way in a classroom. 'Oh yes, we read together every day,' she would say, flicking her hair, and the teacher would nod approvingly and put a big green tick on her mental clipboard.

'Don't wanna go to the library,' said Freddie. 'I'm hungry.'

'Tough,' said Pippa. 'We won't be long.'

Norm got up from his desk when she pushed open the door. 'Need a hand?' he called, coming forward.

'I'm in, thanks.' Pippa piloted Ruby in a curve, just missing the corner of the *New Books* section, and parked her in the children's corner. 'Freddie, why don't you get, let's say three books, and bring them to me at the desk.'

Freddie flung himself on a bean bag and flicked moodily through the book box.

'I was wondering when I might see you,' said Norm, leaning against the edge of his desk, large hands gripping the wood. 'Although it isn't as if you'll need books to keep you busy at present.'

Pippa shook her head. 'Far from it.'

'Any thoughts?' he asked, in an undertone.

'Muuuuuuum, I've read all these books,' Freddie called, in the weary tone of a boy with no new worlds to conquer.

'Maybe find a book with more pages?' Pippa called back. 'Not really,' she murmured to Norm. 'You?'

Norm shook his head. 'I'm not seeing the motive,' he said. 'And I'm not sure that taking the case out of Much Gadding is helping.'

'That's more or less what — PC Horsley said,' Pippa agreed.

Norm gave her a sidelong glance. 'When did he say that?'

Pippa shrugged. 'Just the other day.'

Norm was silent for perhaps half a minute. He looked as if he was working out a division sum in his head. 'Pippa, I advise you not to encourage Jim,' he said, at last.

'Who, me?' Pippa said, as innocently as she dared.

'Yes, you.' Norm frowned at her. 'The last thing this village needs is a promising young policeman like Jim Horsley getting transferred, or worse — and there is plenty worse — out of impatience.'

'But what if Inspector Fanshawe doesn't solve the case?' asked Pippa.

'Some murders do remain unsolved,' said Norm. 'And perhaps the near-certainty of losing a good local policeman isn't worth the slim chance that he might, with the assistance of a sharp amateur, be able to do what the whole of Gadcester police can't.'

'I don't know what you mean,' said Pippa, turning away. 'Freddie, have you found any books yet?'

'Nooooooo,' said Freddie. 'I'm still looking.'

'One thing I will tell you, though, and whether you pass it on to the police — of any shape or size — is up to you.' Norm looked stern. 'Susan told me that there was no way the council would have approved Green Construction's planning application. Not on the meadow. And Tony Green almost certainly knew that. So if preventing the build was the motive, someone's gone to a lot of trouble for nothing. I suggest that you go and help your son.' He sat at his desk again, and pulled his ledger towards him.

Duly dismissed, Pippa went and did what she was told. But while she helped Freddie search, at intervals retrieving Ruby's pram toy, Pippa's mind clicked and whirred like a clockwork mouse. She had no idea what Norm's revelation meant, but there was something to it. Of that she was absolutely sure.

# CHAPTER 17

Imogen didn't speak until they had strapped the children into their carseats. She took a couple of steps away from the Mini, giving Pippa a significant look all the while. 'What did you think?' she muttered.

Pippa made a face, and shook her head. No words were necessary. She got into the car, switched the radio on, and let the music do the talking. Apart from anything else, she needed cheering up.

To be fair, she had had less invested in Upper Gadding Primary than several of the playgroup parents. She didn't particularly want Freddie to go to a faith school, and Upper Gadding would have meant two half-hour round trips every day. Plus hanging-around time, of course. But she had still, sort of, hoped that the school might be an alternative to Much Gadding.

It had started well. The school was in an original, unextended late-Victorian building, and — *and* — it had its own car park. The Much Gadding mums (and a lone dad) gathered on the tarmac outside the door, trying not to look as if they were peering in. They were early, of course, and congratulated themselves silently on this, exchanging glances as frazzled parents, towing their offspring, hurried through the gate.

Ten minutes after the open morning was due to start, when even the latecomers were getting restive, a bored-looking member of staff let them in. She could have been a teacher, or a teaching assistant, or anyone, as she didn't introduce herself; the only clue to her official status was the lanyard round her neck. 'Open morning's in the hall,' she said. 'That way, down the right-hand corridor to the end.' And she hurried away.

The gaggle of parents eyed each other uncertainly. 'Do you think we should sign in?' said one. 'I mean, it's a school, and fire regulations —'

A faint rude word came from the office behind the reception desk, and another lanyarded woman shot out. 'Yes, sign in here,' she said severely, tapping a large book. 'Who let you in?'

'Um, someone?' said Pippa.

The woman clucked and raised her eyes to the ceiling, then watched them all sign in, beadily. 'Don't forget your car registrations,' she said. 'If you've blocked anyone in, you'll have to move.'

'Can we go to the open morning once we've signed in?' asked Sam.

'Yes, it's in the hall,' said the woman, as a small child shot into view behind the glass panel of the left-hand door, followed a second later by a woman who, from her expression and the tone of her (perhaps fortunately) muffled voice, seemed rather irate.

The woman caught sight of the group, and almost stood to attention. Then she opened the door, said 'I'll be right with you in two minutes', and closed it again.

Pippa and Imogen looked at each other. 'Should we wait, or go down?' said Pippa.

'I'm not sure,' said Imogen, shifting from foot to foot. 'To be honest, I'm a bit scared.'

The irate woman turned out to be Miss Trimble, the headteacher. 'Just dealing with a small matter,' she said breezily, as she walked them to the hall. Behind a closed classroom door Pippa heard chatter and the raised voice of a teacher. 'We're a busy school, and some of our pupils are more challenging than others.'

Pippa surveyed the scene as she pushed Ruby, with Freddie's hand firmly under hers on the pushchair handle. The school corridor seemed to have the original wall tiles which were a dull institutional green, the colour of murky pond-water. No artwork brightened the walls, and while some of the classroom doors had pictures stuck on, the general effect was drab.

The school hall attempted to make up for this, with freestanding poster boards filled with photographs of the children doing PE, singing, heads down writing in books. There were a few samples of work, but not many.

'Miss Braithwaite's class will come in a minute to sing to you,' said Miss Trimble, looking at her watch. 'They should be here by now, in fact. I'll see what's keeping them.' And she strode off, her shoes squeaking on the parquet floor. The speed of her exit suggested that whatever the delay, she didn't expect it to be good news.

A few minutes later a ragged line of glum children filed in and droned through three nursery-rhyme style songs to a recorded accompaniment, staring anywhere except at their audience. Everyone clapped dutifully, and the children scurried away.

'We've opened up a couple of classrooms so that you can see the children's work,' said Miss Trimble, brightly. 'Follow me.'

*At last,* thought Pippa, *something useful.* But the two classrooms chosen were the oldest classes, year 5 and 6, and Pippa had no means of judging whether what she was seeing was good, bad, or somewhere in the middle. She considered checking the school's SATs results when she got home, then dismissed the idea. Freddie was going to this school over her dead body.

The open morning dragged on till half-past eleven, punctuated by a lacklustre gymnastics display, a dramatic performance which, they were freely informed, was recycled from Class 4's recent school assembly (Pippa pitied the parents who had had to not only sit through it but presumably also appear delighted), and the occasional far-flung scream.

Pippa dropped Imogen and Henry off, and watched them in. Then she drove thoughtfully home. 'What did you think of the school, Freddie?' she asked, looking in the rear-view mirror.

Freddie's mouth turned down. 'Our school is nicer. Why did we go to that one, Mummy?'

'To see what it was like.' Pippa concentrated on getting the Mini through the ford without mishap. She glanced to the right as she came out, and nearly swerved onto the wrong side of the road as her hands followed her eyes.

The meadow entrance by the ford, which had been sealed off with blue-and-white police incident tape, was open again.

Pippa righted the Mini, and tried her brakes just before the point where the main footpath to the meadow opened onto the road.

That entrance was open, too.

'Why do you do that, Mummy?' asked Freddie.

'Do what?' Pippa replied, guiltily.

'Make the car go slow after we go through the water.'

'Oh. Hang on.' Pippa negotiated the roundabout. 'I put the brakes on so that if there's any water left in them it comes out, and then the brakes will work properly when we do need them.'

'Ohh,' said Freddie. She wasn't convinced he'd understood a word she'd said, but she'd done her best. Probably better than the teachers at Upper Gadding Primary, judging by that morning's experience.

Pippa drove home, changed Ruby's weighty nappy, secured her in her bouncy chair, popped a DVD on, and set about making spaghetti bolognese. The children deserved a nice lunch after such a miserable morning. Plus she and Simon could have the rest for dinner, quite possibly with a glass or two of red wine and in Pippa's case, a full and frank unburdening of their morning at Upper Gadding. She chopped onions and garlic, got them frying, and threw in the various components, walking through to the lounge every so often to make sure no riots were taking place. It felt relaxed, therapeutic, after the stress and poverty of the morning. *Is poverty the right word? It seems so harsh.* But she remembered the bored little faces, the discontented expressions, the little boy banging the door desperate to get out. She sighed, mouthed *Over my dead body*, and opened the cupboard for the spaghetti jar. As she drew out a thumb-and-fingerful of the long, thin, brittle strands, the missing police tape came to mind.

The police had finished with the meadow.

What did that mean? Had they got all they could from it?

Pippa, spaghetti in hand, looked at the pan and realised she'd done things the wrong way round. There was no point getting the spaghetti until she had boiling water to put it in. And the sauce wasn't anywhere near ready. She sighed, and laid the spaghetti on a piece of kitchen roll. That was what came of getting distracted.

*Are we getting distracted?* Pippa pushed the thought away as the casual *we* made her face warm. Unless it was the heat coming from the stove.

*He has a girlfriend. I meant it in a work partner sense.*

*See, you're getting distracted by THAT now —*

'Mummy, when's lunch?' called Freddie. 'We're hungry.'

'It's coming, Freddie,' called Pippa, pushing her slightly damp fringe out of her eyes. 'It's coming.'

***

'So how was the school?' asked Simon, almost as soon

as he got through the door. He had texted earlier, and Pippa had replied *Tell you later :-(*

'When the kids are in bed,' she replied. 'Freddie wasn't impressed.'

'If he doesn't like it, the pair of us wouldn't be able to drag him there.' Simon's hand went to his shirt collar, felt the absence of tie since it was Friday, and undid a second button instead as an acknowledgement of the weekend having arrived.

'How was your day?' Pippa asked.

'So-so. Lots of talking, not much doing.' He made a face. 'Same as most days. You?'

'School visit, came home and made spag bog — which we're having later — took the kids to the park for a run around. Oh, and Lady H rang.'

'Lady H *rang*? What, herself?'

'She wanted to know what's happening about the concerts. Basically, she told me to crack on.'

Pippa had missed Lady Higginbotham's initial call, since she was lifting Ruby into the small swing at the time. It was only half an hour later, when she had sat the children down for a snack break and pulled her phone out to check for Upper Gadding-related messages, that she saw the missed call and voicemail. *Exactly what I need*, she huffed to herself. A*nother distraction*. She pressed *Play* and put the phone to her ear. After a longish pause, Lady Higginbotham spoke.

'Um, hello Pippa, this is June Higginbotham speaking. I'm, ah, a little concerned as I haven't heard from you this week regarding the Proms, and I haven't seen anything in the press. Please could you let me know where you're up to? Um, you know my number. I think. Or, well anyway, it's oh-one-' And the message cut off.

Pippa returned the call during Ruby's nap time. 'Higginbotham Hall, Mrs Harbottle speaking.'

'Oh, hi Beryl, it's Pippa.'

'You took your time,' said Beryl. 'I'll go and see where she is, and then put you through.'

There was a wait of perhaps two minutes before Pippa was connected. 'Ah, Pippa, hello,' said Lady Higginbotham. 'I take it I caught you at a bad time earlier.' Her voice sounded calm.

'I was at the park with the children,' said Pippa. 'We went on a school visit in the morning.'

'I see,' said Lady Higginbotham. 'Anyway, about the concerts. Could you tell me how things are progressing?'

'Well,' said Pippa. 'To be honest I haven't done much to promote them yet, what with the murder. It doesn't seem like the right time.'

'Mm. But can we wait for the right time? Is there ever a right time?'

Pippa wasn't sure what to say to that, so didn't.

'I mean,' Lady Higginbotham continued, 'if we postpone the concerts, we'll have to wait until next summer really. And I have building work to pay for. So I think we should press on. It might cheer people up.'

'You don't think it's a bit . . . insensitive?'

There was a pause, and Pippa held her breath. 'No I do not,' said Lady Higginbotham, and she sounded as close to cross as Pippa had ever heard her. 'The concerts were planned well before that young man got himself murdered. It has nothing to do with him. We should all just move on.' Another pause. 'So if you could get moving on this, Pippa, I'd appreciate it. If not, then I shall make alternative arrangements.'

The silence hung for what seemed like a very long time before Pippa spoke. 'I'll get moving on it. But if ticket sales don't match your expectations —'

'I'm sure you'll do your best, Pippa,' said Lady Higginbotham. 'I'll let you get on. Goodbye, now.' And the call ended.

'So you're going ahead?' Simon asked, with a look she couldn't quite interpret.

Pippa shrugged. 'Lady H is going ahead. I'm just doing her bidding.'

Later, over dinner, Pippa told the tale of their visit to Upper Gadding Primary. 'So Much Gadding all the way, then,' said Simon, sitting back. 'That place sounds dreadful.'

'Its Ofsted rating was satisfactory,' said Pippa. 'I mean, that was a few years ago, but still…'

'You get a feeling for a place,' said Simon. 'Freddie will be fine at Much Gadding. He'll have his friends there, it's a few minutes' walk. It's the sensible choice.'

'I know.'

'You don't seem entirely convinced,' said Simon. 'What's up?'

'It isn't that,' said Pippa. She sipped from her wineglass, thinking. Yes, Much Gadding was obviously a better school, and it ticked lots of boxes, but there was something she couldn't put her finger on…

But if she was going to deliver a successful concert series to Lady Higginbotham, she would have to put everything else aside and concentrate on that…

And then again, if the murder could be cleared up, there was much more chance of getting people to attend the concerts —

'I give up,' said Pippa, taking a gulp of wine and setting her glass down. 'I absolutely give up. It's a complete mess, and if I didn't have to get involved, I wouldn't.'

Simon raised his eyebrows. 'I'm not sure what you're talking about.'

'Neither am I,' said Pippa.

# CHAPTER 18

'So,' said Jim Horsley. 'Any thoughts?'

'I'm not sure,' said Pippa, slowly.

'That means yes, Pippa.' He smiled. 'Come on, out with it.'

Pippa pulled her notebook from her bag and found the notes from her interview with Simon. Briefly, she gave the policeman what she thought were the important points, including what the newsletter article had said, and reported Norm's comment about the planning application.

'That *is* interesting,' said PC Horsley, making a note of his own. 'What do you think?'

'I haven't had much time *to* think,' said Pippa. 'I've spent most of the weekend catching up with the work I should have been doing instead of trying to figure out who murdered Tony Green. Today is the first chance I've had to take a breath, pretty much.'

'Mm,' said PC Horsley, not looking particularly sympathetic. 'So what should you have been doing?'

‘Organising a set of concerts for Lady Higginbotham,’ said Pippa. ‘What did you do this weekend?’ *With your girlfriend, while I was juggling children and phone calls and booking forms,* she added, to herself.

PC Horsley raised an eyebrow. ‘I worked on Saturday morning, and then I did weekend things. The big shop, a walk, a film, Sunday lunch. Why do you want to know?’

‘You asked me, so I thought I’d ask you,’ said Pippa. *And you said I, not we.*

‘Seems reasonable,’ said the policeman. ‘So we now know the planning application wouldn’t have been approved for the meadow, and that Tony Green has been talking about building in the village for at least two years.’

‘Yes,’ said Pippa.

‘But you’re still keeping something back.’ Jim Horsley put his pen down, clasped his hands on the desk, and gave her a steely look. ‘What is it, Pippa?’

Pippa met his eyes and tried to stare him out, but PC Horsley was clearly an experienced starer. With rather nice hazel eyes. ‘I’ve told you what I know.’

‘You have. But not what — or who — you suspect. I’ve been a policeman long enough to know when someone hasn’t told me everything.’

Pippa’s gaze fell. ‘All right,’ she said, and the words snagged in her throat on their way out. ‘I have been thinking something, based on — a few things. It’s kept popping up in my mind all weekend. I hope I’m wrong. I haven’t written anything down, because I so hope I’m wrong. So . . . what I’m about to say is off the record, at least for now.’

‘OK.’ PC Horsley closed his notebook and pushed it towards Pippa. ‘Go on.’

‘I’m worried about Lady Higginbotham.’

‘You’re worried about Lady Higginbotham?’ He could barely keep the incredulity out of his voice. ‘Go on.’

‘She rang me on Friday. She still wants to stage the concerts, even after what’s happened. And when I asked if that was a good idea, she didn’t seem to care about the murder at all.’

‘Well, that isn’t grounds to arrest her, is it?’

‘There’s something else. She came to the consultation meeting, and you know she’s hardly ever seen in the village. And that isn’t all.’ Pippa told him about her meeting at the Hall, when Lady Higginbotham had shown her the view of the meadow, and revealed her plans to restore the sheds as holiday lets.

‘I see.’ Jim Horsley mused. ‘But Lady Higginbotham couldn’t have done it. I’m pretty sure she isn’t strong enough to fell Tony Green with a weapon. And as we both know, she’s got plenty of swords to hand.’

‘So she could hire someone. And of course she wouldn’t use a sword, she knows we know about them.’ Pippa put her head in her hands. ‘I can’t believe I’m having this conversation.’

‘It is pretty surreal,’ said PC Horsley. ‘But you’ve uncovered two plausible reasons why Lady Higginbotham might have something against Tony Green. That’s more than we’ve managed for anyone else.’

‘It doesn’t seem like much,’ said Pippa.

‘But it’s something.’

'Do you know what's going on at the main station? In terms of the investigation, I mean.'

PC Horsley shook his head. 'No more than the basics. They've interviewed all the people you'd expect — Malcolm Allason, Terry Ransome from the naturalist society, the family, of course —'

'Of course,' said Pippa. 'How are they?'

'Shocked. Upset. Unable to believe it. Like most people are in this situation. But of course they were up north when it happened. They all have watertight alibis, including his fiancée.'

Pippa frowned. 'I thought you said you only knew the basics.'

'I got that from a quick chat with Inspector Fanshawe last time I was over there,' said the policeman. 'It's hardly classified information.'

'I suppose.' Pippa thought. 'So you don't think they've had Lady H in?'

'Why would they? It isn't as if she would seem to have anything to do with it. In fact, you could argue that on the surface, with the concert series, the murder would work against her. It's no wonder they've passed her over.'

'So what should we do?'

PC Horsley pulled his notebook back towards him, eyed Pippa, and pushed it away. 'Investigate further, but quietly. Both of us.' His next words were spoken in an undertone. 'Do you have access to her bank accounts? You could check for any largish sums of money disappearing prior to the murder.'

'Look, Jim,' said Pippa, 'I only go to the Hall for the

occasional meeting. It isn't as if I'm left alone in a room there, or given access to her computer.'

'That's a shame,' said PC Horsley, 'it would have made life much easier.'

'Would it?' Pippa faced him across the desk. 'I'm not exactly comfortable with the idea of snooping in a client's home, you know. And what if I'm wrong? She could probably get *me* arrested. Seeing as all this is unofficial.'

PC Horsley held up his hands. 'Just keep your eyes and ears open, then, and I'll do any requisitioning that needs to be done.'

'Fine,' said Pippa, the word shooting out of her more quickly than she had intended.

PC Horsley shot her a surprised and slightly hurt look, as if her reply had stung him. 'You don't have to be involved, if you don't want to be,' he said.

'It isn't that.' Pippa rummaged in her brain for the right way of expressing it. 'But — you're doing your job. I'm supposed to be helping Lady H, and I'm doing the exact opposite. Plus if she finds out, and I'm wrong, my career's probably finished —'

A loud knocking sounded at the front door of the station.

'I'd better go and see who that is,' said PC Horsley. 'Stay put, it's probably a random caller.'

He went through to the counter area, and the knocking, if anything, increased in intensity. 'I'm coming, I'm coming!' he called, and Pippa heard the bolt being drawn back. Then nothing, except footsteps entering. A man, from the sound of it. Probably someone reporting a lost item, or handing something in.

The next noise was the counter flap thumping into place. *Good.* PC Horsley must have got rid of whoever it was.

The door opened, and Inspector Fanshawe stepped in. 'Good morning, Mrs Parker. Do you know, I had a funny feeling I'd find you here.' While his words were light, urbane even, the tone they were spoken in was not, and neither was the expression on his face.

Pippa closed her mouth, opened it to speak and, finding no words there, closed it again.

'I'm glad we didn't need to break the door down,' said the inspector. 'PC Gannet is in the car, and we have the necessary equipment in the boot, but I'd rather not damage police property.'

'Where — where is PC Horsley?' Pippa asked, her throat dry.

'Behind the counter, doing his job,' was the crisp reply. 'Being a community policeman.'

'Should I go?' Pippa made to get up, but Inspector Fanshawe held up a hand, and her blood froze.

'No, you can, ah, *stay put.*' His eyes gleamed.

'You bugged the room,' Pippa whispered, and her heart went into freefall.

'Yeeees,' said Inspector Fanshawe, taking a seat and stretching his legs out. 'Yes, we did.'

Pippa waited for the inspector to say more, but he sat nonchalantly rearranging the objects on the desk. 'What happens now?' she ventured.

He looked up. 'We'll listen it back, of course, and make

a note of what was said, and anything that we ought to follow up.' A pause. 'We might transcribe it formally, if we feel it's necessary.'

'We?'

The corner of his mouth turned up slightly. 'I suppose it's a royal we.'

'What about PC Horsley?'

One eyebrow lifted. 'What about him?'

Pippa shrugged, and closed her mouth. She wasn't going to say anything that could get either or both of them into trouble. More trouble. She watched Inspector Fanshawe, who watched her back with apparent unconcern.

The clock ticked round. A minute, and another.

Inspector Fanshawe sighed. 'I haven't got all day to sit here and wait you out, you know.' He got up and opened the door into the office. A moment later PC Horsley appeared. 'Take a seat,' said Inspector Fanshawe. 'No, next to Mrs Parker. I'll be back in a minute or two.' He strolled into the office, and the main door closed with a click.

PC Horsley fetched a chair and placed it perhaps two feet from Pippa's, then sat down. 'Well,' he said. His tone was flat, but his face spoke volumes.

'They bugged the room,' said Pippa.

'I wondered.'

'What do you think he's doing?'

'I'm not sure,' said Jim Horsley, grimacing. 'And I don't particularly want to speculate on the matter.'

Pippa checked the clock. Five to twelve. 'Whatever it is, I hope it's quick,' she said. 'I need to get Freddie at half past. Not to mention Ruby.'

They didn't have to wait long. The door of the station creaked open, then closed smartly, and the inspector's measured steps approached.

Pippa swallowed as the door opened. *At least he's alone*, she thought. *At least he hasn't brought PC Gannet to witness whatever he's going to do.*

Inspector Fanshawe approached the desk. 'Excuse me,' he said, and reached underneath, bringing out a small black box which looked like a component of the desk itself. The inspector brought it almost to his nose, screwing his eyes up to focus. He prised it open, and took out what looked like a SIM card.

'There,' he said, putting the bug on the desk. Pippa wasn't sure whether to feel relieved or even more alarmed. The inspector took a seat on the opposite side of the desk — PC Horsley's usual place.

'So,' he said, putting his elbows on the desk and leaning forward, as if settling himself in. 'I've told PC Gannet I'll be a few minutes, and then we'll head back to base.'

Pippa let out the breath she had been holding, very slowly.

'You needn't think you're off the hook. Either of you.' The inspector gave both of them a stern look. 'PC Horsley, you knew perfectly well that this case was under Gadcester, and there was no call for you to be sticking your nose in.'

'Sir,' said Jim Horsley, eyes front.

'Mrs Parker, I believe I made it clear when you came in to give your statement that if you came up with any ideas concerning the case, you were to report to me or PC Gannet.'

Pippa squirmed.

'Did I or did I not make that clear?'

'You did, Inspector Fanshawe.'

'I thought so,' he said, as conversationally as if he were confirming that she took milk in her tea. He sat for a moment, apparently lost in thought, then seemed to snap to attention. 'Anyway, we haven't long. Mrs Parker, what are your childcare arrangements today?'

'Um, I have until just before half twelve, that's when preschool finishes.' Pippa began to wonder if she were in some sort of dream, although she couldn't be sure whether it was hers or Inspector Fanshawe's.

'Right. When could you next be free?'

'Well, usually I only have Monday mornings without the children —'

'Could you arrange something?'

'Um, I could ask my mother-in-law, or one of the other mums —'

'Good. Do that, and report back. Jim, I take it you won't mind a change of base for a while.'

'Does that mean I'm not in trouble, sir?'

'I haven't decided yet,' said the inspector. 'But if you agree, you're likely to be in substantially less trouble.'

'Then I agree, sir.'

'Good. I'll tell Gannet the news, and then we can get going. Mrs Parker, I expect you to be in touch shortly.' And the inspector walked briskly out.

Pippa and PC Horsley exchanged glances. 'What just

happened?' asked Pippa.

'I'm not quite sure,' said PC Horsley. 'So far it's a good deal less painful than I was expecting.' His smile was lopsided. 'Let's hope it stays that way.'

# CHAPTER 19

PC Horsley came to collect Pippa from the waiting room, looking considerably more friendly than PC Gannet had done. 'Should I ask what you had to do to come here this morning?' he asked, as they walked along the corridor together.

'Put it this way,' said Pippa, 'if my mother-in-law ever needs an organ donating, she'll be on the phone to me.'

To be fair, Sheila had said little when Pippa had asked her to collect the children from playgroup on Tuesday morning and entertain them for a couple of hours. Her face, however, had said more than enough. 'And what will *you* be doing, dear?'

'I've been called back to Gadcester station,' said Pippa, hoping that would pass muster.

'Oh dear,' said Sheila. 'Did they say why? I do hope Inspector Fanshawe won't be nasty to you again.'

'So do I,' said Pippa.

'Do you think they . . . *suspect* you of something? I

don't know, withholding evidence?' Sheila let the words hang in the air, like a noose.

'I just hope they aren't planning to torture me. After all, they need to save something for next time.'

Sheila looked even more disapproving. 'You're taking this very lightly, I must say.'

'Gallows humour,' said Pippa. 'It keeps me from worrying about it.'

'You're so brave,' said Sheila, patting her shoulder. 'And it's a good thing that they seem to be proactive. I was wondering if they'd stopped investigating, seeing as nothing's happened for days.'

'Mmm,' said Pippa. 'Anyway, I'll take these two away and let you have some peace. Say bye-bye, children, you'll see Granma tomorrow.'

'Can we have fish fingers?' asked Freddie. 'With beans?'

'We'll have to see,' said Sheila, warily.

***

PC Horsley took Pippa to a square, well-lit room. On one wall was pinned a map of Much Gadding, with the meadow outlined in red. Photographs of the body, mercifully face down, and the surrounding area were pinned around the map, with arrows leading to the correct locations. It was eerily similar to what Pippa had imagined.

'Where's Inspector Fanshawe?' Pippa asked. 'Can I sit anywhere?'

'You can,' said PC Horsley. 'He's gone to see Lady Higginbotham.'

‘He hasn’t.’ Pippa’s knees trembled and she dropped into the nearest chair.

‘Mm-hm. He was very interested in our conversation yesterday —’

‘Don’t remind me. That was one of the worst shocks of my life.’

‘It wasn’t great for me either,’ said Jim Horsley, with a wry smile. ‘At the moment I’m just relieved that I still have a job and my freedom.’

‘Could he really…?’

The policeman nodded. ‘I’m pretty sure I haven’t shared anything confidential with you, but he could certainly have found enough to keep me under investigation for a good long spell, and possibly get me dismissed.’ He exhaled, gazing into the distance. ‘Luckily for me, he’s so short of resources that he chose to get us on board instead.’

‘So . . . what’s he doing at the Hall? Did he say?’ asked Pippa.

‘I don’t think he’s going to cuff her and bring her in, if that’s what you’re worried about. He’ll have a word about the concerts, and the likely public reaction —’

‘Oh God, she’ll know I’ve got something to do with it —’

‘Not necessarily. After all, you’ve been promoting the concerts on social media. So, anyway, his plan is to probe her reason for pushing on with the concerts, and see if anything comes to light there. I offered to come too, but he figured that she might talk to him more easily if he went alone.’

'Oh well, if she never speaks to me again I guess I can find other clients,' said Pippa. 'So what are we meant to be doing?'

'He didn't leave precise instructions,' said PC Horsley. 'In your case, you could be reading the information they've compiled about Tony Green, or the interview transcripts —'

'I'll start with Tony Green,' said Pippa. Reading interviews with people she probably knew felt a little too much like peeping through their windows.

PC Horsley opened the top drawer of the desk and passed her a buff folder. 'There you go.'

'I thought they only had these in films,' said Pippa.

'All based on us, you see.' He grinned, then got another folder from the drawer and drew out its contents.

Pippa opened her folder. Inside, arranged in plastic wallets, was a miscellany of photographs of Tony Green as child and adult, newspaper cuttings, printouts of web articles, and neatly-typed pages presumably done by the admin team. She flicked through the photographs, and stopped when she came to a school picture. *Gadding Magna High School, Class 9B, 1995.* Tony Green was easy to spot, and exactly as Simon had described. Shirt half-out, baggy trousers (not in a fashionable way), tie hanging crooked, and hair past his shoulders. Tony Green himself, though, was grinning in a manner which suggested that he didn't care a bit. And he looked much happier than the other teenagers with their forced smiles or attempts at cool.

She sighed, and pulled out a photocopy of a school report from the same year.

*Anthony is enthusiastic about biology, but his written work is not up to the same standard as his responses in class.*

*Anthony has no aptitude for mathematics; in fact he seems to delight in getting his sums wrong, since he makes such a variety of errors in every piece of homework he submits.*

*I have rarely taught a boy whose written work is so appalling — and yet he has a real gift for drama.*

Pippa raised her eyebrows, and turned over more pages. Eventually she came to the piece of paper she had been expecting.

*Having conducted a range of tests, there is no doubt in my mind that Tony is moderately to severely dyslexic. I recommend that the following measures be put in place…*

'I thought so,' she said.

Jim Horsley looked up. 'You thought what, Pippa?'

She tapped the paper in its plastic sheath. 'Tony Green was dyslexic. I was reading his school report and it felt so obvious.' She frowned. 'Why didn't his teachers pick it up sooner?'

PC Horsley shrugged. 'It's a busy school, no doubt, with lots of kids. Probably easier for the teachers to assume it's carelessness or stupidity.'

Pippa studied the report. 'But this says he was fifteen when he was diagnosed. So it probably affected his GCSE results.'

The policeman put his papers down. 'Do you think it has anything to do with his murder?'

Pippa shrugged. 'I feel sorry for him. And amazed that

he did as well as he did.' Then she smiled. 'At least he got to go and do a speech at his old school, so they did acknowledge him in the end.'

'Maybe that's why he wanted to build at Much Gadding,' said PC Horsley. 'To make a point. Make his mark on the place.'

'It's possible. But…'

'What?'

'Why did he choose the meadow? I mean, there's other land available. He must have known that people would make a fuss — the archaeologists and nature types. In fact, I'd have thought he would be one of the people who, if he'd stayed, would have protested.'

'Never even thought of that,' said PC Horsley. 'Maybe it ties in with the making his mark thing. Slap bang in the middle of the village. Not half a mile outside.'

'True,' said Pippa. 'The thing is, he knew he'd be unlikely to get planning permission. So why bother?'

'Unless he had somewhere else in mind all along, and proposing the meadow would make Plan B seem more appealing.'

'Ooh, that's devious,' said Pippa.

'It's business,' said Jim Horsley, with a brief grin. 'Tony Green may have come across as Mr Eco-Friendly, but he had a profit to make, too.'

'I suppose.' Pippa frowned. 'But I wonder…'

'What do you wonder?' Jim Horsley asked, looking puzzled.

Pippa thought, then sighed. 'I don't know.'

Two raps on the door, and it opened immediately

afterwards, with Inspector Fanshawe behind it. 'And another door closes,' he remarked, suiting the action to the word.

'No luck, sir?' asked PC Horsley.

'I didn't expect her to fall to her knees and beg for mercy,' said the inspector, with a sardonic twist to his mouth. 'But it didn't take long to work out that Lady Higginbotham's got nothing to do with the matter. Stick the kettle on, would you.' He flung himself into a chair and swivelled repeatedly in a small arc, like a metronome set to fast.

'Sorry,' said Pippa. 'I really wasn't sure.'

'Nothing to be sorry about,' said the inspector. 'She just couldn't have done it.'

'Did she have an alibi?' asked PC Horsley. 'She could have hired someone —'

A short bark of laughter erupted from the inspector. 'No she couldn't. Lady Higginbotham's absolutely flat broke.'

Pippa gaped at him, and out of the corner of her eye she saw that PC Horsley looked, if not astonished, more surprised than he usually managed. 'How do you know?'

'How do you think?' Another aggressive swivel. 'She told me. This is in confidence, you understand.'

'Of course,' said Pippa and PC Horsley, simultaneously.

'She's barely got enough left in the bank to run the Hall and pay the staff. She showed me her bank statements for the last few months — and no, there are no mysterious payments or withdrawals in cash at any time around Tony Green's murder, so that rules her out.' Inspector

Fanshawe's rocking slowed to a gentler rhythm. 'Basically, if the concerts don't meet your forecasted profit, Mrs Parker, she'll have to sell the Hall, because she can't afford to keep it.'

Pippa stared at him, and as she did a series of clips played in her brain. Lady Higginbotham raising money for the church spire when her own home was at risk; the peeling wallpaper; her pride at the view from the morning-room window; her determination to get the damp sorted out and the roof watertight… 'I can't believe she didn't tell me,' she muttered. 'And I can't believe I didn't work it out.'

'She only told me because I got a tiny bit official with her,' said the inspector. 'We go back a fair way, June Higginbotham and I.' Pippa raised her eyebrows, but he said no more.

'Maybe I should go and see her,' she said, closing the buff folder. 'I feel terrible. I ought to apologise.'

'No need,' said the inspector. 'If anything, she wants to apologise to you for not listening to your objections. "I should have taken Pippa's advice," she said. So I guess you're even.'

'I just wish she'd told me,' said Pippa. She paused. 'So does that mean the concerts are off again?'

'Probably.' Inspector Fanshawe paused at the halfway point of his arc. 'I suggested she get independent financial advice, rather than trying to manage alone.'

'OK.' Pippa exhaled. 'That makes it even more important that we solve this murder.'

'Like it wasn't important before,' remarked the Inspector, with a grim smile on his face.

'You know what I mean,' said Pippa. She put the buff folder on the desk, stood up, and looked at the map on the wall. The exits from the meadow were marked with red arrows, and she touched each in turn.

'We've examined them,' said the inspector. 'And Jim took photos. Didn't find anything significant. It hadn't rained for a while, so no convenient muddy footprints. No unusual sole patterns. No strange marks.'

'No…' said Pippa. 'But all these exits to the meadow come out at a road.'

'Yes, they do,' said the inspector. 'Your point being?'

'Whoever did it would have to leave either by the ford — and cars would be passing then — or higher up, at the Polly's Whatnots entrance. It would definitely have been getting light by, say, seven. Alternatively, you could cross the meadow and come out at the side of the Riverside Bistro — but cars would be going past with their headlights on, and you'd be spotted. The only other way would be to go through the river — and I think it's deep there — or through the back entrance of one of the shops.'

'Already thought of those,' said the inspector. 'The river's five feet deep at that point, and more importantly, ruddy freezing. And we interviewed the shopkeepers, who were all safely tucked up in their own beds at that time, with families prepared to swear to it. So unless the murderer decided to hang out in someone's backyard for a bit with their weapon, and then leave when it would be even busier…'

'And no-one saw anything from the upstairs of the cottages?'

Inspector Fanshawe shook his head. 'The place was carefully chosen. There's a group of trees near where the body was found which would completely shield it from the cottages. Whoever did it planned it.'

'They must have,' said Pippa. 'They can't have had any blood on them. There's no way out of the meadow where they wouldn't risk seeing someone — and if you caught sight of someone spattered with blood, especially at that time of the morning, you'd be suspicious. So whatever they used to kill Tony Green enabled them to do it at arm's length.'

'*And* it was something they could hide easily,' PC Horsley added. 'Because they took it with them.'

The inspector sighed. 'The more I see of this case, the more impossible it gets.' He rose from his chair and wrote on the nearby whiteboard: *Long-handled (telescopic?), heavy yet easily concealed weapon.*

Pippa and PC Horsley exchanged glances. 'Once we've eliminated the impossible…' said Pippa.

PC Horsley sighed. 'Ruddy amateur detectives.' But there was a definite glint in his eye.

# CHAPTER 20

'How was it?' Sheila asked, in an undertone. 'Were they . . . *all right?*'

'Yes, they were fine,' said Pippa, feeling slightly guilty. 'How were these two?'

'They've been ever so well-behaved,' said Sheila. 'I got some fish fingers and they ate every bit, with bread and butter and peas. Oh, and tomato sauce. I think I got most of it off.'

'Thank you so much for minding them,' said Pippa. 'I do appreciate it.'

'Oh, don't worry,' said Sheila. 'Although it was rather short notice . . .'

'I know, I'm sorry —'

'Not that it's your fault, of course,' said Sheila. 'I'm tempted to ring Inspector Fanshawe and ask him what he thinks he's doing, persecuting a young mother who clearly isn't involved —'

'Best not,' said Pippa. 'I gather he's got a lot on his

plate.' Which wasn't exactly a lie, given the portions of fish and chips he and PC Horsley had brought from the canteen.

'I wonder if they'll find the murderer,' said Sheila, dreamily. 'Have you had any more ideas, dear?'

'I'm chewing it over,' said Pippa.

***

'Can we have pudding?' Freddie asked, when they were pulling away from Sheila's house.

'Pudding?' Pippa would have turned round if the Mini hadn't been moving. Trust Freddie to wait until she couldn't react fully.

'Granma said pudding was for tea-time. Didn't she, Ruby?'

A squeak from the other side of the car indicated that Ruby was prepared to corroborate Freddie's statement.

Pippa sighed. 'Grandma does have a point, and at her house it's her rules. However, I could support pudding at lunchtime — mainly because I'd like some. How about we go home, drop the car off, and get a treat from the tearoom?'

'Yay!' There was a definite jerk from the back of the car as Freddie threw his arms up. 'You're the best mummy ever!'

'I know,' said Pippa, feeling anything but. The best mummy ever would probably not have told a half-truth to her mother-in-law to skip off and play police officers, or fill her kids with sugar and fat as a reward. At least the walk into the village would repair the damage a little.

Two iced biscuits and a Bavarian slice later, the trio

emerged from the tearoom. Pippa felt a tiny bit nauseous — it had been a nice pastry, but also rather large. 'Would you like to play on the green?' she asked, hoping that a few minutes' sit down on the bench would settle her stomach a bit. Plus just sitting and thinking, instead of cudgelling her brain for ideas, would be more of a luxury than the Bavarian slice.

'Hello,' called a voice.

The sun was already low in the sky, and Pippa had to shield her eyes to make out the smallish woman standing in front of her. Even so, she was struggling to think who it might be.

'We met at the primary school,' said the woman. 'Emma Knight.'

'Ohh. Yes, of course. Miss Knight. I'm sorry, I'm terrible with faces.'

'It's Ms, but don't worry about it. No, really. If Mrs Jackson can't get it right then there's no reason why you should.' Emma Knight was smiling, but her eyes weren't. 'Did you enjoy the tour?'

'I did, yes. Now I've been on another visit, that puts it into perspective.'

'Indeed.' Freddie had stopped playing and was staring at them. 'And what did you think? Did you like our school?' she called over.

Freddie nodded until his head looked in danger of coming off. 'Can I come?'

'Ooh, it isn't up to me,' said Emma Knight. 'If it was, I'd let you come.'

Freddie threw up his arms and did a lap of honour

round the duck pond.

'I bet you say that to all the children.' Pippa smiled.

'Well, I would. I'd like us to expand to two-form entry.' She sighed. 'Anyway, back to it.'

Pippa looked at her watch. 'But it's half past three, haven't you finished?'

Ms Knight grinned. 'I wish. Lesson plans to go through, resources to dig out, books to mark. I only came out to get medals from Polly's Whatnots.' She dipped a hand into the brown paper bag she was holding and dangled a medal on a red and blue ribbon. 'I thought we had lots, but apparently not.'

'The case of the missing medals,' mused Pippa.

'Excuse me?' Emma Knight's brow furrowed a little.

'Sorry, I thought it sounded like the title of a mystery.'

The teacher laughed. 'Maybe you should see if the library has it in stock.'

Pippa grinned back. 'Maybe I should.'

***

The library was pleasantly warm after the growing coolness on the green. Norm was talking to someone by his desk, his back to Pippa.

*Shame*, she thought. *I could have told him that actually the gamble paid off.*

Except that it hadn't yet, as they hadn't solved the case.

Pippa parked Ruby in her usual spot, and amused herself by scanning the thriller and mystery shelves for any books with *medal* in the title. There weren't any, but still…

Her eyes flicked up and down the shelves, seeking clues. *Death in the Clouds, The Pale Horse,*

*Sparkling Cyanide —*

*Why did so many of them use poison?*

*Duh, because Agatha Christie knew her poisons,* Pippa told herself. Any thug could bludgeon someone to death. Poison required a bit of knowledge.

But Tony Green's murderer wasn't a thug. They had chosen their weapon with care, and so far, they'd got away with it.

*So someone who wasn't a thug, pretending to be one…*

Pippa leaned round the bookcase to see what the children were doing. Freddie, bless him, was showing a picture book to Ruby, turning the pages slowly and pointing. It must be the good influence of Miss — *Ms* Knight. Beyond, Norm was still talking, but had moved round slightly, in the manner of someone ending the conversation, and Pippa could now see that he was talking to Malcolm Allason.

*Nothing unusual in that.*

Malcolm raised a hand in farewell, and ambled to the door carrying two hardback books. He caught sight of Pippa, standing at the shelves, and a troubled expression crossed his face before he said hello. He didn't slow down, which Pippa took to mean that he didn't wish to talk to her. *Not surprising, really.* By the door he stooped to pick something up between thumb and forefinger, examined it for a second, and put it in his pocket. Then he pushed the door open, and left.

Pippa approached the desk. 'Is he all right?' she asked quietly.

'Malcolm?' Norm picked up the book which

presumably Malcolm had returned — *An Archaeological History of South Gadcestershire* — and moved to the shelves. 'He's still a bit shaken, as you'd expect, but otherwise he seems reasonably well.' He slotted the book back into place, and Pippa wondered if it would move again that year.

'Did he mention — you know?'

Norm swung round to face her. 'No, he did not.' His voice was low, but the disapproval in it was very clear. 'Malcolm is by way of being a friend of mine. And I thought I told you that encouraging Jim Horsley wasn't a good idea.'

'Well, it turns out you were wrong,' said Pippa, and stalked off. 'Come along Freddie, time to go.'

'But we're reading!' said Freddie.

'*Fine*,' snapped Pippa. She took the book from him, marched to the desk, and thumped it down. 'Freddie would like to borrow this book, please,' she said, looking anywhere but at Norm.

Norm slowly opened his ledger, found the right page, uncapped his pen, and wrote down the book details. 'Anything else?' he asked. 'A volume on anger management, perhaps?'

'Not today. Thanks for your help,' said Pippa, as sarcastically as she could manage, and wheeled Ruby off at such a pace that the wheels skidded on the carpet tiles.

'Pippa, I didn't —'

Pippa spun the pushchair round, barged the door with her bottom, and exited. Not the most dignified departure ever, but certainly satisfying, as the door creaked shut behind her.

'Mummy —' Freddie's little face wore an expression of complete confusion. 'Why are you cross? And why did we have to go?'

'We didn't have to go,' said Pippa. 'I chose to go. And I'm cross because — because *people*.'

Freddie seemed to accept this as a valid explanation. 'Look!' He pointed, with the whole extent of his arm, to a figure ambling a few metres ahead of them. 'There's the funny man from the library.'

'Don't point, Freddie, it's rude,' Pippa said on autopilot, before seeing that yes, indeed, the round-shouldered, slightly stooped figure of Malcolm Allason was not far ahead, carrying the books he had borrowed. 'But yes, it is the man from the library.' Malcolm stopped dead, crouched for a moment, then straightened.

'I *told* you,' said Freddie, triumphantly. 'I think he's dropped something.'

Pippa slowed down. Was he going home? She presumed he lived in the village. That would fit with a morning stroll on the meadow, at any rate. If he had travelled there — She shook her head impatiently. Perhaps she was getting a bee in her bonnet about the case.

Malcolm Allason walked slowly alongside the green towards the war memorial, which he studied for perhaps half a minute. Then he kept going, past the chippy and Dot the florist's, past the Riverside Bistro, looking at the ground most of the way —

'Where are we going, Mummy?' asked Freddie, in his not-indoor voice.

'We're just having a little walk,' said Pippa, but their quarry had stopped again, and was poking something lodged in the cobbles of River Lane with the toe of his shoe. Would he ever get home?

'Mummyyy…' Freddie whined.

Pippa jumped as her mobile rang. She parked Ruby and rummaged in her bag. *Sam.*

'Oh hi Pippa!' Sam half-shouted, over shrieking and yelling in the background. 'I tried texting but you must have missed them. I would have said at playgroup but you went out early…'

'I was, um, I had an appointment,' said Pippa.

'Oh OK. School stuff?'

'Kind of,' agreed Pippa, crossing her fingers.

'Anyway, I'm going to The Manor tomorrow morning — they're doing a show-round. Would you like to come?'

'The Manor?' Pippa hadn't even considered The Manor, partly because it was a private school but mostly because it was the far side of Gadcester. She closed her eyes for a moment and saw straw boaters.

'I *know*, but the photos on the website are amazing. So what do you think?'

'Tomorrow morning? What time?'

'Eleven,' said Sam, and Pippa could hear the beam in her voice. 'Enough time to drop Livvy at preschool, get over there, quick tour and questions, then back for pick-up.'

'Ohhh…' Pippa lowered her voice. 'So you're not taking…'

‘Absolutely not, not after the last one,’ Sam said. ‘She was literally traumatised.’

‘I see what you mean,’ said Pippa, slowly. Ahead of them Malcolm was crouching, fishing between the cobbles. ‘Yes, I’m in. Thanks for letting me know. Um, see you at preschool?’

‘Great, see you then!’ Sam bawled. ‘Sorry about the noise, I’m at soft play.’ And the phone cut out.

*What about the case?* complained Pippa’s inner detective.

*I can’t go to the police station tomorrow anyway, I’ve got Ruby.* Pippa’s inner detective retreated, grumbling that she could have found a way if she’d really wanted to.

*Finding a school for Freddie is important too*, she added.

Freddie tugged at her hand. ‘Can we go home, Mummy?’ he asked. ‘I want to finish the story.’

Pippa sighed, and watched Malcolm straighten up, examining an object in his palm. ‘So do I, Freddie, so do I.’

‘That doesn’t make sense, Mummy,’ he said, as she turned the pushchair round.

‘No,’ said Pippa, ‘it doesn’t.’

# CHAPTER 21

'It's beautiful, isn't it?' whispered Sam, as the choristers in their surplices, bathed in coloured light, sang their little hearts out.

'Yes,' Pippa whispered back, 'it is.' *And too good to be true*, her sceptical self added. Heaven only knows what Freddie would have made of it.

She had given Sam a lift, since Ruby's pushchair wouldn't fit in Sam's boot, and the pair of them had gasped as they turned into the drive of The Manor School. It was grander than Higginbotham Hall, and, of course, in considerably better repair. The lawns were green and manicured, and a fountain tinkled in front of the warm, wide stone building. To top it off, two children were waiting at the top of the steps for them, a boy and a girl. 'Welcome to The Manor School,' they said, in unison, and Pippa tried not to think of horror movies. At least they weren't wearing straw boaters.

The children introduced themselves as Pepita and

Jonathan, head girl and head boy, and conducted them ably round the school, pointing out artwork, classrooms, the honours boards, and a range of team photos. The Manor seemed to encourage sports from dressage through fencing to rowing. 'We go boating on the river in summer,' said Pepita, 'but the little ones start off on the lake.'

'The lake?' asked Pippa, feeling slightly dizzy.

'Yes, past the kitchen garden,' said Jonathan. 'It's two feet deep, so it's ideal for confidence-building.'

And of course they grew their own vegetables.

Everyone they met, from teachers to grounds staff to the smallest pupils, seemed lovely, and they were all achingly polite. Sam wandered about, mouth half-open, as if she were in a dream. *Perhaps we are,* thought Pippa. *Maybe we've gone through some sort of portal and we're both dreaming the same vision of the ideal school.*

Only, for her, it wasn't. She just couldn't see Freddie there, becoming an impeccably-mannered child who would no doubt sail into the diplomatic service or the UN or the higher regions of particle physics. Plus the fees were eye-watering, even for day pupils. 'Bursaries are available,' Pepita said kindly. 'They have booklets in the office.'

Sam wiped away a tiny tear as Pepita and Jonathan waved goodbye from the steps. 'It was so lovely,' she sniffled.

'Don't forget the open day effect,' said Pippa, backing the car cautiously out of its space. The last thing she needed was to ding one of the posh cars parked nearby. Even the gravel crunched expensively. 'Those two are probably pulling each other's hair and eating sweets now.'

'You know they aren't,' scolded Sam.

'I know, they're perfect.' Pippa sighed. 'Anyway, it was fun.' She reached the end of the drive and indicated right.

'It was.' Sam delved into her bag, brought out a booklet, and began to flick through it.

'Is that about the bursaries?'

'Mm-hm,' said Sam, then dropped it on her lap. 'Who am I kidding,' she said. 'It's miles away and really expensive. Even with a bursary.'

'Livvy will be fine, wherever she goes,' said Pippa, her eyes on the road as she negotiated a sharpish bend in the narrow lane.

'I don't know,' said Sam. 'She isn't very confident, and a place like that…' She twisted in her seat to look back, though they were well out of sight of it.

'Realistically, though, who from Much Gadding will be able to send their children there? Hardly anyone. So all Livvy's friends would live somewhere else.' Pippa steered round another bend. 'Probably in palaces. And imagine this road in rush hour.'

Sam shuddered. 'And in winter.'

'They probably drop them off in the chopper when it snows,' said Pippa, and they both snorted.

'OK,' said Sam. 'What *are* you going to do about schools?'

Pippa considered. 'Keep looking. But Much Gadding primary's still my favourite so far.'

Sam made a face. 'I suppose.'

***

Pippa parked at preschool and checked her phone. A

rare text from Lady Higginbotham: *Hello Pippa, I have been thinking about the proms and perhaps you are right about putting them on hold.* She opened the message to reply, then saw the time change from 12:28 to 12:29. 'Better pick them up,' she said.

Sam unbuckled her seatbelt. 'Will you tell Freddie what we've been doing?' she asked. Her cheeks were pink.

'No,' said Pippa. 'Will you tell Livvy?'

Sam shook her head. 'No way.'

'You ladies look as if you've been on an outing,' said Dawn, when she opened the door.

'Oh no, not at all,' said Sam. 'We haven't gone anywhere.'

Confusion spread over Dawn's face. 'But you must have gone somewhere,' she said, 'I saw the car pull up.'

'Freddie!' Pippa called, to cause a diversion. 'Have you had a nice morning?'

'Mummy!' Freddie charged over like a miniature rhino and whumped into her side. Pippa remembered Pepita and Jonathan, standing so nicely on the steps, and grinned. She'd rather be whumped into any day of the week.

Livvy got up and wandered over, her big blue eyes focused on Sam's face. 'Hello, pet,' said Sam, and folded her in a big hug. Livvy's thumb stole into her mouth.

'Has Freddie been good?' Pippa asked Dawn.

'Played nicely, ate everything, said please and thank you.' Dawn ticked the evidence off on her fingers.

'That'll do.' Pippa ruffled his hair.

'I was *super* good,' said Freddie, puffing out his chest. 'Does that mean I can have a treat?'

'I hope you didn't behave nicely *just* in the hope of getting a treat,' Pippa said, mock-severely. 'But yeah, probably.'

***

Pippa threw her music folder on the passenger seat of the Mini and prepared to leave for choir practice. She had replied to Lady Higginbotham with a neutral message which hopefully left things open for the future, and also managed to text Jim Horsley while making a cup of tea. *Any more news?* She almost put an *x* on the end, out of habit, and swore under her breath as she caught herself just in time. That definitely wasn't the sort of impression she wanted to give. She even checked her sent text, to be absolutely sure she hadn't slipped up.

His reply came five minutes later. *Still plugging on, still weapon-hunting. No joy from allotments. Morale low. Tea supplies dwindling. Maybe we should resort to doughnuts. Jim*

She smiled to herself. *You should listen to me, see. P*

*Anything at your end?*

She shook her head before realising that wasn't going to work. *Nope, have been viewing school.*

*MG?*

*No, posh school.*

That was a point, she should text Simon and tell him how the morning had gone. She found his number and texted *Manor v nice but can't see F there.*

Another almost instant reply. *Why not? x*

She considered her answer. *Too . . . punts on the river and silver trophies x.* Then she went to the fridge for milk.

A reply was waiting on her return. *But surely posh is good?*

Pippa's thumbs flew over the letters. *I'm sure it is but can't see me mingling with the gentry on the croquet lawn and cheering Freddie on at his polo match x*

She clucked, and got a spoon to fish her teabag out of the cup. The tea would probably be strong enough to put hairs on her chest.

*Me neither — Jim ;-)*

Pippa stared at the phone in horror, then unlocked it and scrolled. Yes, she had just sent a daft text with a kiss on the end to the wrong man. She laid the phone on the worktop, and took a couple of deep breaths before picking it up again.

*I'm sorry that text was meant for someone else. Pls ignore. Pippa.* She checked it twice, and pressed *Send*, then put the phone face down. Her cheeks were burning, and she put her hands on the cool plastic bottle, then on her face.

The phone buzzed. Pippa turned it over, her heart thumping.

*I like the sound of silver trophies but not if we have to sell a kidney each. Speak later? x*

Pippa felt half relieved, half-disappointed. *Exactly. I'm at choir tonight but we can talk over afterwards if you want x,* she replied. She took the tea through to the sitting room, and punished her indiscretion with undivided attention to a whole episode of *SuperMouse*. When it was over she put her phone in the cutlery drawer to stop herself from checking it, and played Ludo with Freddie. They were halfway through the game when Ruby woke from her nap, and keeping her entertained while finishing the game kept Pippa occupied for another half an hour.

Pippa only remembered her phone when she took her empty mug to the kitchen. She opened the dishwasher and slotted her mug into the top tray — no doubt Sheila would be scandalised, but Sheila wasn't there — then retrieved the phone.

*OK*, said the message on the home screen.

*Probably for the best*, thought Pippa. What exactly had she been hoping for, some sort of mild text flirtation? Frankly, she had better things to do, like decide what variant of breaded-things-and-veg the children would eat tonight, or cook a proper meal for herself and Simon, instead of the two-person lasagne which was sitting in the freezer. Or try harder to find a school for Freddie that she was completely happy with.

*Or solve a murder.*

*With Jim Horsley.*

And Pippa felt her cheeks warm up all over again.

***

'Well good heavens, look who it is!' Jen exclaimed as Pippa sidled into the church hall. 'I did wonder when we'd next see you, Pippa.'

'Sorry,' Pippa muttered, as she walked into the ranks of the choir.

'If you're rusty — which you *might* be — pop yourself next to Edie. Right, warm-up.' Jen tapped the stand with her baton. 'Arpeggios.'

Pippa was glad to lose herself in the simplicity — or so

it felt — of trying to keep her place and not hit the wrong note at the wrong time, or indeed any time. Jen was right. She *was* rusty. And with Christmas concerts on the way, not to mention the prom if it ever happened, she couldn't let the choir down. Not if she wanted to stay. Suddenly her music was blurry, and her throat hurt. She blinked once, twice, and rubbed her eyes surreptitiously, and mouthed along until the song came to an end.

'All right, not bad,' said Jen. 'Let's take a break. Doing OK, Pippa?'

'Fine,' Pippa croaked, keeping her head down.

'That isn't a sore throat I can hear, is it?'

Pippa swallowed. 'No.'

'Good. That'd be the last thing we need.' Pippa felt the air around her cool slightly as people edged away.

She stood in the queue behind Edie. Perhaps tea — no, perhaps *coffee* would help. She thought of the tea steeping in her kitchen while she had sent the fateful text, and shuddered.

'Are you poorly?' asked Siobhan, touching her sleeve. 'You look a bit shivery.'

'I think the weather's getting colder,' said Pippa.

'And damper,' said Gerry, turning round. 'It'll be winter before you know it. Time for me to get my hat and scarf out and check the tyres on the float. And time for you to swap your golf bag for your knitting needles, Edie.'

'Get out of town, Gerald,' said Edie, comfortably. 'All-weather driving range at Gadcester, don't you know.'

'I wouldn't know,' said Gerry. 'I don't have posh hobbies.'

'Just singing a cappella,' said Edie. 'Nothing posh about that, eh. Now face the way you're going, or you'll knock the table. Health and safety.'

Gerry muttered under his breath, and did as he was told.

Pippa got herself a coffee, and the bitterness matched her mood. What was the point of running round every primary school in Gadcestershire when the council would decide anyway? Why should she abandon her children, and wind up her mother-in-law, in order to try and solve a murder which even the police couldn't get to grips with? 'Oh, I give up,' she said to herself.

'Never say that,' Edie scolded, as she passed. 'You're an alto, and altos aren't quitters. Just keep trying.'

'I didn't mean that,' said Pippa, but Edie was already out of earshot.

'Places, everyone,' Jen called. Pippa drained her coffee cup and aimed for the bin, but missed. It rolled slowly, as if mocking her, right to the back of the chairs, and Pippa had to crouch and lean and strain to retrieve it. But as she let go of the cup and it dropped into the bin, she gasped.

Jen tutted as Pippa hurried to her place. 'More haste, less speed,' she said, tapping the stand. 'Right, from the top again.' She frowned at Pippa. 'Are you sure you're all right?' she asked. 'You look as if' — she checked herself — 'well, I don't know.'

*I do*, thought Pippa. *As if I've seen a ghost.*

# CHAPTER 22

Afterwards, as Pippa said her goodbyes and walked to her car, she wondered why on earth she hadn't made an excuse and left after break. Perhaps it had been the thought of more people staring, more remarks from Jen, and possibly another telling-off at the next rehearsal which had kept her in her place.

And also force of habit.

Pippa sank into the driver's seat of the Mini and, for no reason that she knew, locked her door. Then she got out her phone.

*I think I know what the weapon was…*

She typed for some time, correcting the occasional wrong guess from her phone, read the text, checked it was going to the right person, and pressed *Send.* Then she had another thought: *And find out which trousers MA was wearing when he found the body.*

A reply flashed up on Pippa's phone as she started the car. *I assume both of those texts WERE for me. V v interesting. Can you come in tomorrow?*

Sheila's likely expression flashed through Pippa's mind. *Not sure. I'll try.*

*Please do — J*

She put the phone in her bag and backed out of the empty car park. Jim Horsley was probably sitting on a sofa right now, possibly next to his girlfriend. Or else in the pub, with his phone sitting next to a pint and a packet of crisps. She shook her head and tried to concentrate on the road. *How will I act normal in front of Simon with all this churning round in my head?*

The answer came as she was waiting at the lights.

*You won't.*

***

'How'd it go?' Simon called from the sitting room. 'There's a bottle of red open in the kitchen if you want.'

Pippa briefly considered a glass of wine, then rejected it on the grounds that her head was spinning enough without additional help. She went into the sitting room, dropped her bag and folder by the sofa, and sat down facing Simon.

He didn't look up at first, as a car was rolling over and over on the TV. When he did, though, the sight of her face made him grab the remote and hit the pause button. 'What's up?' he asked. 'Whatever is it?' He got up and sat beside her, but even when he put an arm round her, it seemed to be happening to someone far, far away.

'I don't know where to start,' she said. 'But I think I know who killed Tony Green, and how.'

Simon drew back a little, and his face was very serious as he studied her. 'Have you told the police?'

‘I’ve texted Jim Horsley. It only came to me at choir, and of course it needs checking out —’

‘Of course.’ The warmth of his arm was beginning to make itself felt, and Pippa’s shoulders relaxed a little. ‘Is there anything I can do? You don’t have to tell me who you think it is,’ he added quickly. ‘I have a distinct feeling I don’t want to know.’

‘He asked if I could go up to Gadcester station tomorrow. I don’t know if you could put a good word in with Sheila, but I can’t take the children —’

‘I’ll take carer’s leave then. I can ring in the morning.’

Pippa looked up at him. ‘Are you sure?’

Simon nodded. ‘If you’re sure that you’re on the right track. And you look as if you’re sure.’

Pippa sighed, and leaned into his arm. ‘I wish I wasn’t. But it all makes sense. Horrible, horrible sense.’

***

‘Are you sure you’ll be all right?’ Pippa asked Simon, as she picked up her bag and keys.

‘I’ll be fine,’ said Simon. He leaned forward and murmured in her ear. ‘Are you sure *you’ll* be all right?’

‘Daddy!’ Freddie shouted from the dining room. ‘Ruby’s dropped her toast!’

‘I’ll be right there,’ called Simon. ‘You look exhausted, Pip.’

‘I’ve had better nights’ sleep,’ Pippa admitted. She had spent an hour the previous night browsing the internet, seeking evidence which could support — or disprove — her theory, and possible lines of enquiry to follow up. Her notebook was groaning with question marks.

'OK. Well, drive carefully. I don't want you to ring me from the police station in the wrong sort of way.'

'I know.' Pippa kissed him on the cheek. 'Thank you.' She stepped back. 'You will text or ring if anything's wrong, won't you?'

Simon grinned. 'Anyone would think you didn't trust me. Now go and do your thing.'

'I — I need to say goodbye to the kids again.' Pippa went through to the dining room and kissed both children on the top of the head — everything else was likely to be too sticky. 'Be good for Daddy, and I'll see you both later. Love you.'

'Where *are* you going, Mummy?'

'I'm . . . doing something different today. You'll still go to playgroup, don't worry. Just with Daddy.'

Freddie, his face confused, opened his mouth and Pippa fled.

***

*I'm here*, Pippa texted from the car park. Her knees wobbled and her stomach churned almost as much as they had the first time she had arrived at Gadcester police station.

But this time she was here to do a job.

Jim Horsley was waiting for her at reception. 'Here.' He passed her a *Visitor* badge on a lanyard. 'I've already signed you in.'

'Thanks.' She looped the badge over her head, and fell into step beside him.

'I hope you don't mind, but I forwarded your texts to Inspector Fanshawe,' he said. 'We've been in since seven, working on it.' His voice was calm, but his posture, the way he walked, the slight curve of his hands as he paced, suggested that he was holding himself in, conserving his energy.

'I spent some time on the internet last night, following up,' said Pippa, pulling out her notebook as they reached the office. 'This is what I got.'

Inspector Fanshawe was writing on the whiteboard when they entered. Pippa read the neat, squarish capitals, and swallowed. The thoughts that she had texted last night were becoming more and more real by the moment.

The inspector drew a box round his words. 'It's looking plausible, very much so, but we need something conclusive. This makes sense to me, but unless we can get a firm sighting, or prints, or DNA, I'm loth to proceed.'

'I've been thinking,' said Pippa. 'We've been wondering how the person managed to take the weapon with them without anyone noticing it. If it's what we think it is, the answer is obvious — it was hiding in plain sight. But there would be traces.'

'There would,' said the inspector. 'But would they still have it?'

'The weapon, yes,' said Pippa. 'The other, I doubt it. It would be almost impossible to clean.'

'They've probably dumped it,' said Jim Horsley. 'We can check the tip, and waste ground in the area.'

'They'd get a new one,' said Pippa. 'People would notice if one was missing. I've made a list of every possible retailer within twenty miles. There aren't many.' She found the page in her notebook and held it up. 'They could have bought one online, but that would leave a trail.'

'Looks like we have a plan, then,' said the inspector. 'Jim, you take the tip, and see what you can dig up. Maybe literally. If you can get it, get it. I'll ring round the retailers and see what they can tell me, go over if I have to.'

'What about me?' asked Pippa.

The inspector smiled. 'I'd like you to call on Malcolm Allason. I think he'll take the request better from you.'

***

Malcolm opened the door himself, peering round it suspiciously. His expression brightened a little when he saw who it was — or who it wasn't — then settled into querulousness. 'Mrs Parker, isn't it?'

'That's right,' said Pippa. 'Could I come in? I wanted to ask you something.'

The door didn't move. 'What did you want to ask me?'

'Could I come in?' Pippa repeated. 'It isn't something that I want to ask on your doorstep.'

'Who is it, Malcolm?' a voice called from above their heads. 'It isn't cavity wall again, is it?'

Malcolm's eyes were on the swinging badge which Pippa had forgotten to remove. 'No, dear,' he called, then looked back at Pippa. 'Do you have authority to come here asking questions?'

Pippa sighed. It all seemed so much easier on TV. 'It's me or the police. Inspector Fanshawe thought you might prefer me, but I can ring and ask him to come —'

'No, no, don't ring him,' Malcolm gabbled, his eyes round with panic, and pushed the door open.

The table in the narrow hall was cluttered with objects;

oddments in bowls and boxes, groups of items laid out on mats. Malcolm stepped into a sitting room and held the door for Pippa. 'Could my wife join us?' he asked. 'I — I got a bit nervous when I had to go and talk to the police.'

'Of course she can,' said Pippa. 'She can probably help.'

Malcolm walked to the door and inclined his head upwards. 'Judy,' he called, 'could you come down?'

'I'm on my way,' a voice called, and Pippa heard first a low muttering, and then the creak of the stairs.

'Take a seat,' said Malcolm. 'Would you like a cup of tea?'

'I'm fine, thanks,' said Pippa. Her stomach was already doing a spin cycle, and the thought of adding tea into the mix wasn't a pleasant one. She took in the room. There were things everywhere — collections of pottery fragments, bits of twisted metal, old coins. It was like the cleanest junk shop she had ever seen.

'Are you in here?' said the voice which had called from upstairs, and a neat, slim woman in beige trousers and a peach blouse came in and sat gingerly in the armchair. 'Sorry it took me so long, my hip is playing up. Rain's on the way, for sure.' She stared at Pippa. 'Do I know you?' Her tone wasn't exactly hostile, but neither was it friendly.

'My name's Pippa Parker, and I live in the village,' said Pippa.

'Oh,' said Judy. 'Pippa Parker.' Her voice was definitely swinging towards hostile. 'I've read about you in the paper. Organising things.'

'I called because I noticed something the other day, and

it could be important.' Pippa's eyes flicked to the crammed shelves. 'I happened to walk behind you in the village the other day, Malcolm, and you picked up a couple of things on the way.'

'There's no law against it,' said Judy, crossing her legs.

'It isn't hoarding, or anything like that,' said Malcolm. 'We're quite able to manage.' He peered at her badge. 'Where did you say you came from?'

'There's nothing wrong with picking things up,' said Pippa. 'I assumed it was just a habit. A completely harmless habit.'

'That's right,' said Malcolm. 'All of history is under our feet, you know.' He looked shyly proud.

'I bet you've found some really interesting things,' said Pippa.

'I have,' said Malcolm. 'I found a Roman silver bracelet in a field once, you know. It's in Gadcester Museum.' He smiled, and the tension in the room eased a little. 'Now, what did you want to ask me?'

'I wondered,' said Pippa, 'what trousers you were wearing on the day you found Tony Green.'

Malcolm goggled, then turned to his wife. 'Can you remember what trousers I was wearing, dear?'

'The green corduroys,' said Judy. 'Your odd-job pair.'

'That's it!' said Malcolm. 'But why do you want to know?'

'Um, in case you picked anything up while you were out.'

'Oh!' said Malcolm, then frowned. 'I don't think so… At least, I don't remember. But would I, after all that?'

'I'll go and find them,' said Judy. 'Come with me.' She stood, using the arm of the chair to help, and made her way to the door. Her progress up the stairs was achingly slow. 'I hid them,' she said. 'I didn't want Malcolm upset again, and…' A sudden laugh. 'I must admit that I'm trying to get rid of the horrid things. Getting Malcolm to part with anything is very hard.'

At the top of the stairs was a polished chest of drawers. Grumbling a little, Judy bent and opened the bottom drawer, then lifted a folded blanket. 'Here they are,' she said, handing Pippa a pair of worn, faded bottle-green cords.

'May I?' asked Pippa. She pulled on a plastic glove, and rummaged in the left-hand pocket, then deposited the contents on the chest of drawers.

An irregularly-shaped black stone, a dirty fragment of something or other, some loose change.

*Now the other pocket…*

More coins, a folded receipt, an elastic band, a train ticket, a pink plastic golf tee, and a washer with a bolt through it.

'Well,' said Judy, 'good luck with that lot.'

Pippa produced a plastic bag from her pocket and dropped the strange collection in. 'I'll ask Malcolm if he remembers where he picked them up, and then I'll be on my way.'

'Thank you, dear,' said Judy. 'Although now you've reminded him of those trousers…' Her mouth twisted a little.

'Sorry,' said Pippa, contritely.

Malcolm studied the collection of items. 'I remember the receipt,' he said. 'I picked that up outside the bakery. I meant to put it in a bin, but I must have forgotten.'

'Would you mind if I took these with me?' asked Pippa.

Judy laughed. 'Please do.'

'If you can make anything of that, you should join the force properly. It's beyond me.' Malcolm shook his head. 'Do you need anything else?'

'I don't think so,' said Pippa. 'Thank you very much for your help.'

'That's all right,' said Malcolm. 'You were much less scary than the real police.'

'Good,' said Pippa. She stood, shook both their hands, and Malcolm saw her to the door. She waved as she drove away, and hoped, though she wasn't sure why, that Judy hadn't noticed her reaction when one particular thing dropped onto the chest of drawers.

# CHAPTER 23

'Do I look OK?' Pippa asked, scrutinising herself in the wardrobe mirror.

'You look fine,' said Simon. 'Although I'm not sure what you *should* look like, to be honest.'

'I suppose I'm aiming for harmless,' said Pippa.

'In that case,' said Simon, 'you're fine.' He kissed her. 'Is your phone fully charged, and not on silent mode?'

Pippa saluted. 'Sir yes sir.'

'Good. Text me when you've arrived, and if there are any problems, just get out. You're the most important thing.'

'Where's Mummy going this time?' Freddie moaned from his room.

'Mummy's trying something new,' said Pippa, 'and hopefully she'll be back before lunch.'

'Oh,' said Freddie. 'What are *we* going to do, Daddy?'

'We're going to have fun,' said Simon. 'And maybe do some shopping.'

'Food shopping?' Freddie asked suspiciously.

'Maybe —'

'You said *fun!'*

'I'll leave you to it,' said Pippa, kissing Simon once more, and ran downstairs. If she wasn't careful, she'd miss her booking.

The traffic around Gadcester was surprisingly light for a Saturday morning — but when was she ever out of the house this early? Hopefully she wouldn't stick out like a sore thumb, or look too silly, or injure anyone. She had seen the building many times on the approach to Gadcester, but she had never thought she would go inside.

Until now.

She parked — the car park was already busy — and texted Simon. *Here safe, going in x.*

The reply came almost immediately. *Good luck x.*

Pippa texted again. *About to enter. Are you in position?*

She stared at the screen, waiting for the beep, the buzz.

*All in and ready.*

There was nothing for it now. Pippa checked her reflection in the visor mirror, got out, and walked briskly towards the driving range.

'Mrs Parker?' The receptionist checked her screen. 'Yes, I've got you down for bay ten.' Then she looked at Pippa. 'Is it your first time?' she asked.

Pippa nodded. 'Could I hire some clubs? I, um, wanted to try it before I bought a set.'

'Very wise,' said the receptionist. 'You could hire a full set, or you could use a couple that we keep for people to try out.'

'Oh, could I?'

'Sure.' The receptionist leaned over the desk. 'Josh! Could you get this lady some tryout clubs?'

A tall young man with floppy blond hair raised a languid hand, collected three clubs, and brought them over. 'Here you go.' He held them out to Pippa, who wasn't sure how to take them. She'd watched a couple of videos online, but actually holding the clubs felt strange.

'They won't bite!' he laughed. 'Or break. Come on, I'll take you to your bay. Don't forget your balls.'

Pippa stared. 'Excuse me?'

'Your bucket of balls. Small, medium or large?'

'Er, medium please.'

The receptionist reached under the counter and handed over a bucket two-thirds full of golf balls. 'There you go. You can always come back for more. That'll be five pounds, please.'

Pippa held her card against the machine, wondering why on earth anyone would pay five pounds to hit a bucket of golf balls into nowhere. But then some people thought singing was a bizarre hobby. 'Thanks,' she said, and hefting her bucket and clubs, followed Josh to bay ten.

'Are you left or right-handed?' he asked.

'Right,' said Pippa.

'OK, stand this way round then. The ball goes there. Now, side on, feet apart, line your club up, swing back . . . and go.'

Pippa swung the club, and completely missed the golf ball. 'Oh dear,' she said, feeling incredibly incompetent. 'Can I have another go?'

'You can. Line up again.'

This time Pippa managed to connect with the ball, which flew off to the left.

'OK that's better —' A bleep on Josh's belt went off. 'I need to get back to the shop. Keep doing that. Try the other clubs too — the wood is the best one for distance.' And he moved off at a relaxed pace.

Pippa stared at the clubs, trying to work out which was the wood. The man two bays down, who was presumably left-handed as he was facing her, saw her confusion. 'What is it?' he called.

'Which one is the wood?' Pippa called back.

'The one with the biggest head,' he replied, pointing.

'Ah. Thanks.'

The woman immediately to Pippa's right, immaculate in an aqua polo shirt and slim-fitting navy trousers, looked over her shoulder with an incredulous smile on her face. 'You're new, then,' was all she said. She lined her club up, swung, and they both watched the ball fly in a perfect arc before landing near a distant flag.

'Wow,' said Pippa.

'It takes a lot of time, and practice,' the woman said, bending to retrieve another ball.

'Aren't you Mrs Jackson from the primary school?' Pippa asked.

'That's right. And I am also Lady Captain of the Greater Gadding Golf Club.' She lined up and played another ball, which followed exactly the same path as the first.

'So you're very good, then.'

'I try,' she said. 'I'd be playing a round now if the course at Greater Gadding hadn't been a complete bog for days.'

Pippa got a ball and attempted another shot with the wood. This one connected, but the ball shot off to the right this time. Shelley Jackson followed its progress. 'Interesting swing,' she commented.

'It's my first time,' Pippa countered.

'I can see that.' Another perfect shot left the range. 'You should think about lessons, if you mean to continue.'

'Maybe I should.' Pippa retrieved another ball from the bucket. This time Mrs Jackson watched Pippa take aim, and she missed the ball. The corner of Shelley Jackson's mouth quirked up, and she addressed herself to her tee again.

'I believe we've met,' said Pippa.

'Have we?' A pause. 'I'm not sure we have.'

'Yes, I came on the tour of your school a couple of weeks ago. On the day poor Tony Green was found dead.'

Shelley Jackson's shoulders stiffened. 'Oh yes. I'd forgotten it was the same day.' She turned and scrutinised Pippa. 'Now you've said, I do remember you. You had a pushchair.'

'That's right.'

'And did you like the school?'

'I did. Although I'd like it more if it was bigger.'

'Oh yes, you asked me about that, didn't you?' Mrs Jackson's shoulders relaxed a little. 'As I recall, I said that I didn't think it was likely. And I still don't.'

'No,' said Pippa. She had another try at her ball, and

managed to hit it straight this time, though it didn't travel as far. 'And now that the build in Much Gadding isn't going ahead, you could be right.'

'I'm here to practise,' said Shelley Jackson. 'I don't like discussing school matters at the weekend, and I certainly don't want to talk about Tony Green and his housing development. Poor man,' she added.

'Didn't you teach him? At primary school? My husband remembers you, and he was at Much Gadding with Tony Green.'

'I might have done,' said Shelley Jackson. 'Obviously that would have been a long time ago. If you'll excuse me —'

'So how long have you been teaching, Mrs Jackson?'

'Over thirty years, although now that I am a headteacher I am much less hands-on.' She forced a smile. 'I shall probably retire in a few years, and enjoy my leisure time. Including more golf that I am currently managing to play.' She glared at Pippa.

A man in the driving range uniform of forest-green polo and matching cap tapped Pippa on the shoulder. 'Are you managing?'

Pippa smiled. 'I think I'm getting the hang of it.'

A snort came from her right, and Shelley Jackson played another beautiful shot.

'She's ever so good,' Pippa commented.

'Yes, she is,' said the man on Mrs Jackson's right. 'A very strong drive. Impressive.'

Shelley Jackson fetched another ball, and did it again. Pippa could imagine the smug look on her face. Another man in forest green came over to watch.

'Definitely strong enough to kill someone,' commented the man on her right. 'If she had a mind to.'

Shelley Jackson, in the middle of lining up her next shot, froze. 'I beg your pardon?' she said, in a voice as chilly as her posture.

'You did teach Tony Green,' said Pippa. 'And you do remember him, because you attended his speech at the high school two years ago. The one where he said he wanted to build a housing development in Much Gadding. I found a video of it on YouTube, and you're in the audience. Oh, and Tony Green also talked about the obstacles he'd overcome, like his dyslexia. Before his diagnosis he said everyone thought he was either naughty, stupid or both. And that everyone probably included you.'

'I did teach Tony Green,' said Shelley Jackson. 'And you're right, I didn't think much of him. But that's no reason to kill him. Making accusations like that is against the rules here. You should both be thrown out and barred.' She eyed the men in forest green, eyebrows raised, but no-one made a move. 'Fine.' She rammed her club into its cover, dropped it into her golf bag, and hefted it onto her shoulder. 'Don't expect me back any time soon. Or any of my friends, when they hear about this.'

She tried to push past, but one of the men laid a heavy, heavy hand on her shoulder. 'I'm sorry, Mrs Jackson, but you can't leave.'

'What do you mean?'

Inspector Fanshawe took off his cap. 'Shelley Jackson, I am arresting you on suspicion of the murder of Tony

Green. You do not have to say anything…'

His words blurred into the background as Shelley Jackson's expression changed from incomprehension to fear. 'But . . . but…' she stammered.

'Can you hand your bag to the officer, please,' said the inspector.

She unhooked the bag from her shoulder and held it out to PC Horsley. 'Why did I do it, then?' Her tone was almost mocking.

'You were scared,' said Pippa. 'A new housing development would mean more pressure to extend your school. A school where you had resisted change for years, and a school where, perhaps, you felt you were losing control. Questions were already being asked at council level, and Ms Knight had been recruited to the school as a possible successor. With just a few years until retirement, you'd oppose anything which endangered your position. Then along came Tony Green, someone you'd never had any time for as a boy, with his cool eco-ideas. You'd heard him speak at the high school. You knew he could win people over. And you decided to do something about it.'

Shelley Jackson blinked a slow, reptilian blink.

'I don't know how you persuaded Tony Green to meet you at the meadow — certainly there was no meeting in your diary. Maybe you said you wanted to implement green energy for the school, and asked him to show you the development site. He was probably either pleased that you finally respected him, or looking forward to gloating over his victory. And he was off his guard.'

'You have no proof at all,' said Shelley Jackson. 'This

is just speculation.'

PC Horsley held up the golf bag and pointed at the head covers on the clubs. 'I found one of these at the tip,' he said. 'Same make, same colour. It wasn't broken, it wasn't damaged, and there was no obvious reason to throw it away. I've passed it to the forensics team.' He paused. 'Easy to clean a golf club when you get it home. Not so easy to clean the cover you stuffed it into, covered with blood and who knows what else.'

'We also had a chat with Malcolm Allason,' said Pippa.

'That old fool,' muttered Shelley Jackson. 'You probably put words into his mouth.'

'He gave us something better than words,' said Pippa. 'Among the things he picked up that day, just before he came across the body, was a pink golf tee. Bound to have fingerprints on it. I have a funny feeling —'

'Oh shut up,' said Shelley Jackson. 'Just get it over with.'

Inspector Fanshawe raised his eyebrows. 'My pleasure, Mrs Jackson. The car's this way.'

'I have one request,' she said, scowling at Pippa. 'Don't put her in the back with me. If there's one thing I hate it's mindless chatter.'

Jim Horsley made a small noise, then straightened his face as Pippa glared at him. 'Take her away and deal with her, Jim,' she said.

She watched the police officers depart with Shelley Jackson. PC Gannet tried to take Mrs Jackson's arm, but she shook him off and stalked beside him, clasping her elbows.

‘Pleased to meet you,’ said the golfer who had assessed Shelley Jackson’s swing. ‘Dr Watson, forensic medical examiner.’ He held out a hand.

‘Pleased to meet you, Dr Watson,’ said Pippa, shaking it. ‘I won’t make any Sherlock Holmes jokes.’

Dr Watson winced. ‘Please don’t.’

‘Excuse me, have you finished?’ At her elbow was a portly man in a golfing sweater, carrying a large bucket of balls.

‘Yes,’ said Pippa, picking up her clubs. ‘You can have the rest of my bucket.’

‘Not for you, then?’ he asked, looking at the half-full bucket.

‘Not my thing,’ said Pippa. ‘Bit too violent.’

# CHAPTER 24

'Pippa,' said Monika, brandishing her clipboard, 'we have a problem.'

'Oh God, do we?' Pippa halted on her way to the hotdog stand. 'What is it?'

'We are missing a member of Short Back and Sides, and the second half is due to start in ten minutes.'

'Oh.' Pippa smiled. 'He's probably in the loo or getting a drink or something.'

'I told them all to be backstage fifteen minutes before,' Monika insisted.

'I'm sure it'll be fine. If whoever it is hasn't arrived in five minutes, let me know.'

'Very well,' said Monika, with a look that suggested she thought Pippa was being disappointingly lax. 'I shall watch for Jeff. I told the others not to move.'

'Jolly good,' said Pippa, and dashed off to join the growing queue.

Five minutes later, armed with hotdogs, she returned to

the tartan picnic rug. 'Lila, have you seen Jeff?'

Lila shook her head. 'Haven't seen him since we got here, apart from performing.' Her tone was light, and she was smiling, but Pippa sensed that both were for her and Simon's benefit.

'I wonder where he's got to. Here, have a hotdog.' She handed out her spoils, taking care to keep the mustard and ketchup away from her new jeans. 'That's one thing about a night off from the kids, we can eat whatever rubbish we like.'

'True,' said Simon. 'Aren't you joining us?'

'In a minute,' said Pippa. 'I'm going to see if Jeff's turned up yet. I may need to save him from the wrath of Monika.'

'Want me to look after your hotdog?' asked Simon.

'No,' said Pippa. 'I'd like to eat it.'

When Pippa arrived backstage, Monika's face told her immediately that Jeff wasn't there. 'Two minutes,' said Lewis, the group's second-in-command. He frowned. 'I don't think he's ever been late before. He's usually the one rounding *us* up.'

'Hello folks!' said Ritz Robertson, bouncing up. 'Ready to rock and roll?'

'Could you give us a couple more minutes?' asked Pippa.

He grinned. 'Someone stuck in the loo?'

'Possibly,' said Pippa. She hurried round to the lawn, scanning the crowd for Jeff. He should have been easy to spot, with the black leather jacket and quiff, but there was no sign of him. She pulled out her phone and texted:

*Where are you?*

The reply came quickly. *Sorry got held up. Start without me. There in five.*

Pippa stared at the phone.

'Everything all right, Mrs Parker?' It took her a moment to recognise the speaker since she had never seen him out of uniform before — unless you counted the driving range uniform. Jim Horsley was sitting on a fleece blanket, beer in hand, casual in jeans and a dark green sweatshirt. Next to him sat a young woman with brown bobbed hair, wearing jeans, a stripy top, and a fierce expression.

'Um, yes, fine,' replied Pippa, tucking her hair behind her ear. 'Just a small matter of a missing person, but I'm sure he'll surface eventually.'

'Jim, not now,' muttered the young woman, putting her hand on his.

'Well, don't ask me,' said Jim Horsley, looking rather embarrassed. 'I'm off duty.'

'So I see,' said Pippa, to his glass of beer. 'Anyway, I'd better go. Deserters to catch and all that.' As she walked off, Jim Horsley's girlfriend leaned in. He certainly wouldn't get the opportunity to desert.

She arrived backstage to find Monika pushing Ritz Robertson towards the curtain. 'You are late,' she was saying. 'You must go on.'

'Jeff's on his way,' said Pippa, waving her phone. 'He said to start without him.'

Bemusement rippled through the assembled group like a Mexican wave. Lewis stepped forward. 'It'll be fine,' he said. 'You know what to do. We'll open with "When Will I Be Famous". I solo on that, so it'll be less obvious.'

'Break a leg,' said Pippa. 'I'm sure it will be great. I'll clap extra loud.'

Pippa made her way back to the rug as Ritz did his spiel, and sat down next to Simon as the group came on. 'Has he turned up?' asked Simon.

'No, he hasn't, but he says he's coming.'

'Oh, OK.'

'You don't sound very bothered,' she scolded.

'If he says he's coming then he's obviously fine,' he replied, and swigged at his beer. 'Did I see you talking to PC Horsley?'

'You did. And his girlfriend.'

'Oh yes. Remind you of anyone?'

'Not particularly.' Pippa bit into her cooling hotdog and brushed a crumb off her Breton top. Then she glanced at Lila, who was watching the group, mouth pressed closed, and sighed. Everything had gone so well up till now. The event was filled to capacity, Lady Higginbotham was delighted, and she had already booked the damp-proofing people on the strength of the first show. *Don't let me down, Jeff.*

The group began to sing, wearing their usual happy, confident faces, but Pippa could see uncertainty in the way their eyes shifted around the audience. But no-one seemed to notice. People were clapping along, just as always.

The group hit the final chord, and as they did Jeff walked on stage, clapping. While Pippa wasn't an expert lip-reader, she could have sworn that Lewis mouthed 'where were you?'

'Sorry I'm a little late,' Jeff said. 'I had a little something to do which couldn't wait.' The group exchanged glances behind him. 'Anyway, for one night only, I've decided to do a request slot.'

Lewis stepped up beside him and muttered in his ear.

'Lewis has reminded me that we don't do requests.' Jeff grinned. 'It's OK, Lewis, I'm the one making the request.' He turned to face the audience. 'Lila Dawson, would you mind coming up here?'

Lila sat rigid, staring at the stage. 'Go on,' said Simon, nudging her. 'Go and talk to the nice man.'

'What's going on?' she muttered, still not moving.

'All right then,' said Jeff, 'I'll come down.' And as he walked he took a small black box from his pocket. 'Scuse me,' he said, as he weaved between the rugs, tracked by a lone spotlight.

Lila's head turned slowly towards Pippa. 'Did you know about this?' she breathed, her eyes sparkling.

Pippa shook her head. 'Innocent, your honour,' she said, through her grin. 'Although I'm not sure my husband could say the same.'

'I plead the Fifth,' said Simon.

Lila scrambled to her feet as Jeff approached. 'You didn't have to —'

'I've been meaning to for some time,' Jeff said, 'but it was never the right moment. Stuff kept getting in the way. I had to dash off to practice, or I'd worked late, or you'd worked late… And then tonight I realised that if I waited for the perfect moment, I might wait too long. So I went to my flat to get the ring.' He opened the box, and knelt on the grass. 'Lila, will you marry me?'

Lila's smile was dazzling enough to rival the spotlight. 'I need to think about it,' she said. 'Talk about putting me on the spot, Jeff.' Then she pulled him to his feet and threw her arms round him. 'Yes, of course yes!'

And the crowd went wild.

'Did you set this up?' Pippa murmured to Simon, as Jeff and Lila kissed.

'Nah,' said Simon, putting an arm round her. 'I may have undertaken minor facilitation.'

'You old romantic,' she said, and kissed him.

Lila and Jeff came up for air. 'I suppose you ought to go and sing,' Lila said.

'I suppose I should,' Jeff replied. 'Show's back on!' He gave Lila one last kiss and walked towards his grinning and clearly relieved bandmates. Monika, hovering near the stage, looked furious, but she was the only one. Lady Higginbotham, sitting at one of the side tables, was applauding gently, while Beryl Harbottle was dabbing at her eyes with a handkerchief.

Jeff shook Lewis's hand. 'You know that song we tried out, which we all agreed was way too soppy to perform in public?'

Lewis nodded. 'Just this once?'

'Just this once. I'll start us off.' Jeff sang the chorus of 'Marry You' solo before the rest of the group joined in. Even Monika was smiling now.

'It *is* a beautiful night,' murmured Simon.

'Gosh, you really are getting soppy in your old age,'

Pippa whispered back. 'Or else it's the beer.'

'Weeeell…' He squeezed her gently. 'Successful concert, Lila's happy, Jeff's happy, your crafty friend is happy, the school thing is sorted —'

'If Emma Knight stays in charge —'

'She will. And she'll get the school extended.' Simon drank some beer.

'And the police station is staying open after all.'

'Is it?'

'Mm-hm. Jim — PC Horsley texted me. I thought I'd said.'

'Well, that *is* good news, seeing as you can't be expected to fight crime in the Much Gadding area all by yourself. So everything's perfect, except —'

Pippa shot him a look. 'Except what?'

Simon grimaced. 'When Mum finds out that her kind offer to babysit means that she's missed the proposal of the year, she'll kill me. She's only just forgiven *you* for wrapping up another case without her.'

Pippa punched him gently. 'You idiot.'

'Hey, mind the beer!' said Simon, moving his plastic cup away. 'Criminal waste, that.'

'If that's the worst you've got to complain about, you're doing pretty well,' said Pippa, leaning over and swiping the cup from his grasp.

'I ought to have you arrested,' said Simon.

'Or buy me a beer of my very own,' said Pippa.

'I suppose there is that,' said Simon, getting up. 'I'll bring one for Lila too, she's far too starry-eyed to look after herself.' Lila was alternating between gazing at the stage and the ring on her finger. 'Bless.'

Pippa hugged her knees and looked around her. Great music, a happy audience, a marriage proposal, and a cold beer on the way, courtesy of her loving husband. What could be nicer? *Right now*, she thought, *not much.* And as the song drew to an end, she smiled.

# ACKNOWLEDGEMENTS

First of all, thank you to my indefatigable and speedy beta readers: Ruth Cunliffe, Paula Harmon, Stephen Lenhardt and new recruit Joanne Locke, who gets a special thank you for knowing infinitely more about golf than I do!

Another thank you to John Croall, who proofread the manuscript and saved me from any potential medical gaffes.

Big thanks to my husband Stephen Lenhardt for his support. He not only reads the output of my creative labours, but also keeps me fed while I'm not engaged in them. The man's a hero!

Just a quick note here that the schools in this book are in no way based on any schools that I've ever visited or worked in — and the teachers and headteachers are all figments of my imagination too!

And finally thanks to you, the reader. I hope you've enjoyed reading this book, and if you would like to leave a review for it on Amazon or Goodreads, I'd appreciate it very much. Reviews, however short, help other readers to discover books, so authors value them highly. Go on, make me happy!

## FONT AND IMAGE CREDITS

**Fonts:**

MURDER font: Edo Regular by Vic Fieger (freeware): www.fontsquirrel.com/fonts/Edo

MEADOW font: Florabet by West Wind Fonts (freeware): www.fontspace.com/west-wind-fonts/florabet

Classic font: Nimbus Roman No9 L by URW++: www.fontsquirrel.com/fonts/nimbus-roman-no9-l. License — GNU General Public License v2.00: www.fontsquirrel.com/license/nimbus-roman-no9-l

Script font: Dancing Script OT by Impallari Type: www.fontsquirrel.com/fonts/dancing-script-ot. License — SIL Open Font License v.1.10: http://scripts.sil.org/OFL

**Graphics:**

Plan: taken from House Plan by NorasFed (edited to skew design): www.vecteezy.com/vector-art/102534-free-house-plan-vector

Spade: taken from Garden Equipment Vectors by sunshine-91 (edited to broaden spade): www.vecteezy.com/vector-art/96528-garden-equipment-vectors

Houses: taken from Free Townhomes Vector Icons 1 by kangkikur: www.vecteezy.com/vector-art/99456-free-townhomes-vector-icons-1

Trees: taken from Free Tree vector by nightcharges (edited and recoloured): www.vecteezy.com/vector-art/101875-free-tree-vector

Daisies: taken from Flat Flower Vectors by veernavya (edited for perspective): www.vecteezy.com/vector-art/157753-flat-flower-vectors

Cover created using GIMP image editor: www.gimp.org.

# ABOUT THE AUTHOR

Liz Hedgecock grew up in London, England, did an English degree, and then took forever to start writing. After several years working in the National Health Service, some short stories crept into the world. A few even won prizes. Then the stories started to grow longer . . .

Now Liz travels between the nineteenth and twenty-first centuries, murdering people. To be fair, she does usually clean up after herself.

Liz's reimaginings of Sherlock Holmes, her Pippa Parker cozy mystery series, and the Caster & Fleet Victorian mystery series (written with Paula Harmon), are available in ebook and paperback.

Liz lives in Cheshire with her husband and two sons, and when she's not writing or child-wrangling you can usually find her reading, messing about on Twitter, or cooing over stuff in museums and art galleries. That's her story, anyway, and she's sticking to it.

Website/blog: http://lizhedgecock.wordpress.com
Facebook: http://www.facebook.com/lizhedgecockwrites
Twitter: http://twitter.com/lizhedgecock
Goodreads: https://www.goodreads.com/lizhedgecock

# BOOKS BY LIZ HEDGECOCK

**Short stories**

*The Secret Notebook of Sherlock Holmes*

*Bitesize*

**Halloween Sherlock series (novelettes)**

*The Case of the Snow-White Lady*

*Sherlock Holmes and the Deathly Fog*

*The Case of the Curious Cabinet*

**Sherlock & Jack series (novellas)**

*A Jar Of Thursday*

*Something Blue*

*A Phoenix Rises* (2018)

**Mrs Hudson & Sherlock Holmes series (novels)**

*A House Of Mirrors*

*In Sherlock's Shadow* (2018-9)

**Pippa Parker Mysteries (novels)**

*Murder At The Playgroup*

*Murder In The Choir*

*A Fete Worse Than Death*

*Murder In the Meadow*

**Caster & Fleet Mysteries (with Paula Harmon)**

*The Case of the Black Tulips*

*The Case of the Runaway Client*

*The Case of the Deceased Clerk*

*The Case of the Masquerade Mob* (2018)

Printed in Great Britain
by Amazon